time for you

time for you

ELIZABETH DAVIS

Montlake

This is a work of fiction. Names, characters, organizations, places, events, and incidents are either products of the author's imagination or are used fictitiously. Otherwise, any resemblance to actual persons, living or dead, is purely coincidental.

Published by Montlake, Seattle
www.apub.com

Amazon, the Amazon logo, and Montlake are trademarks of Amazon.com, Inc., or its affiliates.

EU product safety contact:
Amazon Media EU S. à r.l.
38, avenue John F. Kennedy, L-1855 Luxembourg
amazonpublishing-gpsr@amazon.com

ISBN-13: 9781662529771 (paperback)
ISBN-13: 9781662529788 (digital)

Cover illustration and design by Elizabeth Turner Stokes

Printed in the United States of America

To my husband, the funniest man I know

Chapter One

Daphne wove through the busy hallway, dodging nurses and skirting an empty bed someone had left in the hallway outside the trauma operating room. Her next patient was a nineteen-year-old who probably needed his stomach pumped thanks to a two-for-one deal on fishbowls at Uncle Pete's Tavern. A dive bar just a few blocks from the university, Uncle Pete's was usually responsible for at least one stomach-pumping admit every weekend, and three the weekends after finals. But this Friday had seen five already, and Daphne was about ready to burn Uncle Pete's down. Or at least write them a strongly worded letter about irresponsible drink specials.

It wasn't that Daphne hated fun, although she'd had several roommates in undergrad who would probably claim she did, along with at least half of the other first-year residents (though at least some of them would say so fondly). It was just that Daphne had always been very focused, and things like "getting drunk because it's fifty degrees for the first time since October" or "getting drunk because midterms are over" or even just "getting drunk because it's Friday" simply didn't appeal to her.

"I hear you're not feeling well," she said brightly, pulling back the curtain around the bed. The boy was clutching a bedpan and moaning while his friend swayed in that drunk-college-kid-trying-to-be-sober-around-real-adults sort of way. The friend was on his phone, a maroon baseball hat twisted backward on his head.

"Any chance he can get out of here soon?" the friend asked. "The Sig Eps are throwing a rager."

Daphne made sure her face stayed neutral, because she had never gone to a single "rager" in college and had always thought they sounded really gross and overwhelming. She had spent those nights studying instead, because Daphne was a woman with a plan and always had been. Daphne had been only six when she and her mother ended up in the ER after a horrible car crash, and Daphne would never forget being so scared and in pain—her leg was broken in two places—while her mom was wheeled into surgery for a busted spleen. It was the ER doctors who had helped soothe her, put her back together, and patched up her mom. Daphne, always a very decisive child, had made up her mind there and then: She would become a doctor and work in an emergency room, providing the exact same comfort and reassurance as those doctors.

Comfort and reassurance she was admittedly struggling to provide at that exact moment, as the patient begged her to discharge him now "before the hot ones are taken."

She knew exactly what he meant, although she wished she didn't. "I don't think I'd advise having buffalo wings when you've been vomiting," she said dryly.

"No, I mean—" he started, but a look from his slightly-more-sober friend cut him off. "Yeah, uh, I guess you're right."

Daphne started asking the patient questions, pausing every so often to let him vomit, and pondered what her college life might have been like if she hadn't been so fixated on becoming a doctor. She had never once let herself get distracted: no partying, no goof-off semesters abroad, none of it. A lot of people thought she was missing out on life, but Daphne preferred to think of herself as pursuing an important goal. Her best friend, Ellie, was just about the only person who thought she was *fun*, and that was mostly because Ellie had also wanted to go to med school.

Daphne finished her exam and confirmed what the nurse had suggested—overconsumption of alcohol requiring a stomach pump. Daphne double-checked with the attending, Dr. Gupta, and then sent the orders for the patient, plus a recommendation to his friend that they *not* attempt any more two-for-one drink deals or ragers for a while, before plunging back into the chaos of an emergency department on a Friday night.

The action was nonstop. Daphne saw another Uncle Pete's fishbowl casualty (twenty-two-year-old female dragged in by concerned friends, fortunately not dire enough for the stomach pump, although she'd have a hell of a hangover in the morning), followed by a motorcycle accident (broken collarbone and road rash), and the usual drips and drabs of people without regular access to a doctor arriving because their conditions, whatever they were, were no longer manageable at home. Vibol was on shift too, and he tossed her a sympathetic yet wry look as he consulted with a nurse.

Eight hours into her shift, with three still to go, Daphne ducked into the supply closet. She shut the door behind her, blocking out the noise of EKG machines, beeping monitors, and calls of various staff to each other for assistance. She took a deep breath, inhaling the antiseptic scent of hand sanitizer.

She liked this. She *did*. Well, maybe not *this* this, but she liked helping people. Just because it was overwhelming sometimes didn't mean she wasn't cut out for it. First year of residency was notoriously awful. Just last week Brittany had ended up crying on Daphne and Ellie's couch about something the chief resident had said to her during rounds. This feeling was totally normal. It had to be. Besides, Daphne didn't like to dwell. She had plenty of experience pushing through something that felt impossible (hello, Organic Chemistry II), so she would buckle down until the life of a resident felt like comfortable tennis shoes instead of stilettos.

A sliver of light poured in as the door cracked open. "Possible appendicitis in bay five, Dr. G," James, the shift's head nurse, said gently. "Twenty-eight-year-old female, stomach cramps and vomiting."

"Be right there." Daphne sighed. She took another shuddering breath, and back out she went.

James's assessment was right. The woman had all the classic signs of appendicitis, so Daphne admitted her and sent her on upstairs for surgery.

During a rare lull an hour later, Daphne leaned back against the wall and closed her eyes, while Ellie sat on an empty bed in the hallway next to her. "I am going to personally murder the owner of Uncle Pete's," Ellie complained. "I've been puked on twice, and I'm on my third set of scrubs."

Getting into the same residency program as Ellie, after their separation for med schools in different states, was the best thing that could have ever happened. As tiring as it was, at least they weren't in it alone. They'd made new friends in the program too, although it didn't quite cure the ache Daphne felt in her chest sometimes, the one that felt like loneliness.

"At least you had time to change. I think I fell asleep on my feet while James was going over a chart. Brittany's so lucky, getting to sleep tonight."

"Dr. Levine, we need a consult in bay four," a nurse called, and Ellie smothered a groan.

"Be right there, Hannah," she replied, and turned to Daphne. "There's some frozen pizzas at home. Can you throw one in if you get off first?"

Daphne nodded and took what felt like her fiftieth deep breath of the shift before returning to work.

◆ ◆ ◆

Ellie got called in on a trauma thirty minutes before they were supposed to get off, so Daphne dragged herself back to their apartment alone. She threw the pizza in the oven, realizing at the last possible second that she'd left the plastic on.

Fire hazard averted, Daphne forced herself to shower—cold water only, so she could stay awake to eat, since the last thing she'd managed was half of a protein bar five hours earlier. If she fell asleep without eating, she'd be even worse off when she woke up. Today had been rough, but Daphne could handle it. Exhaustion was just part of being a resident. They were all constantly tired. In fact, discussing it was probably all the residents' favorite game: *I'm more tired than you and I can prove it.*

Shivering and with soaking-wet hair dripping down her back, Daphne picked at her sausage and red pepper pizza until Ellie burst through the door in her usual whirlwind of activity. Ellie ran through a play-by-play of the end of her evening while downing two slices, then stood from their secondhand table—donated by one of Ellie's many, many aunts—and considered Daphne. "You know, I wish I could be more like you."

"What, cold and clinical?"

"Sure of myself," Ellie countered. "You're exactly where you've always wanted to be, and you're thriving."

Thriving wasn't quite the word Daphne would use to describe herself, but then again, she was bone tired. It was probably just the exhaustion that made her look down and blink back tears. "You're killing it, too," she argued.

"Yeah, but daily I'm like, someone's gonna notice I'm an idiot and fire my ass."

"That's just impostor syndrome talking."

"Or maybe I *am* an impostor," Ellie replied. "Maybe I have you all fooled."

"You don't. Trust me."

Ellie looked like she was about to say something, but she shook her head. "You okay?" she asked after a beat of silence that went on just a little too long.

"I'm fine. Just tired."

"We should do something next time we're both off. Something stupid."

"You of all people know that's not my style," Daphne replied with half a grin.

"Which is exactly why we should do something stupid and impulsive." Ellie dropped a kiss on top of Daphne's head. "You sure you're okay?"

"Positive," she said, and leaned into Ellie's shoulder. "G'night."

"I mean it. Stupid and impulsive. We'll get Michelle and Brittany and Vibol in on it and everything. Soon," Ellie said. "And get some sleep, okay?" she added on her way to her room, leaving Daphne alone under the single light in their kitchen, with nothing but cold pizza and her thoughts for company.

Chapter Two

Daphne checked the time on her phone again and tried not to whip her head around the second the door jingled with a new customer. Behind the counter, a machine hummed as the barista worked on an order, and a group of elderly men held court on the chairs nearest the window. Daphne drummed her fingers on the table and sipped her drink slowly, hoping she wouldn't look impatient if her coffee was more than half-gone before he even arrived. Her date had said he could probably make it by two, but like her, his job could be unpredictable and tough to schedule around, so it really wasn't unsurprising he was a little late.

A half hour is more than a little late, Ellie's voice whispered in her head. *No dick is worth that.* Ellie had slightly different opinions about men and dating than Daphne did, to be sure. Ellie wasn't interested in romance, or dating, or really anything other than friendship and fucking. Which worked very well for her, Daphne had to admit. But that wasn't the vision Daphne had for her life.

She had done her best not to think about romance for the last—well, a lot of years, because she was so sure it would distract her. Daphne didn't need to go all soft and mushy while she was applying to med school, studying in med school, and scoping out residencies. She needed strict, uninterrupted focus.

She wasn't sure exactly why she'd decided the time was right for dating a month ago, after years of self-enforced semi-celibacy. (That guy from that party two years ago only half counted, seeing as only one of them had gotten off, and it sure as hell hadn't been Daphne.)

Her date, assuming he wasn't standing her up, checked all the boxes for a future Mr. Daphne Griffin: tall (six three according to his profile, which meant he probably cleared six feet, once she accounted for the Dating App Inflation that Ellie said was currently running at about two and a half inches); blond (*You sure you won't look like twins?* Brittany had asked, clearly underestimating the key role Peeta Mellark had played in Daphne's middle school life); and the founder of a tech start-up, which meant he was ambitious, just like her.

"Daphne?" a deep voice asked, and she stood up, pleased to find he hadn't been lying at all about his height.

"You must be Anders," she said. He was broad, big shouldered, and thickly muscled. Clearly, he spent a *lot* of time at the gym. Maybe too much. *No judgment. We all have hobbies,* she reminded herself.

There was an awkward moment where they did a little half dance, him leaning in for a hug while she moved out of the way, holding out her hand instead. She was acutely aware of all the times she'd been called *cold*, but Anders let it pass with an easy grin. *One point for Anders.*

"I'll just go get my drink," he announced.

◆ ◆ ◆

He returned soon after, with a mug of tea and a scone. *A* scone. That he put right in front of his chair. "Today's my cheat day. I do intermittent fasting the rest of the week," he explained.

It wasn't that Daphne particularly wanted a scone, but it would have been nice to be asked, that was all. "You were saying you're working on a new app?" she prompted. She had been chatting with Anders for a couple of weeks, so she knew the rough contours of his job, but the specifics, as he'd explained over text, hadn't made a ton of sense to her.

His eyes flashed but his smile didn't waver, and it was over so quickly she decided she'd imagined that split second of annoyance. "It's a podcasting app that uses generative AI," he said.

"How does that work, exactly?"

His eyes narrowed slightly. "Why?"

"Um, because I'm interested? I'm not super familiar with how AI can work to help podcasts, I guess," she replied, a little taken aback by his suspicion.

"Oh." He laughed, and the tension bled away. "You mean you don't get it. Okay."

"What did you think I meant?"

He shrugged and pinched off a piece of scone. "We've got some rivals who are interested, that's all. Can't be too careful, you know?"

Daphne didn't know, quite frankly, but she nodded like thinking she might be engaging in corporate espionage was a super-understandable mistake anyway. *Not everyone clicks right away. I just have to give it a little more time,* she reminded herself. Texting with him had been if not great, then okay enough, so maybe they just needed a little bit of time to warm up to each other again.

Anders started explaining—and explaining. And explaining. As far as she could tell, he was using generative AI to create prompts for podcasters, which he was hoping to sell as a sort of "idea machine" to interested hosts, who would then pay him to also host the podcast itself on the app. Daphne wasn't particularly creative, but she wasn't sure how necessary the artificial intelligence part was to his whole idea, since it was really just a brainstorming session. She stared down into the dregs of her coffee and tossed it back, annoyed to find it had gone ice cold in the past five minutes. Daphne hid her grimace and kept listening, waiting for a chance to ask a question.

The moment finally came. "So, it sounds like this is a podcasting app that also comes with some ideas for them to use?"

Anders sighed, almost imperceptibly. "Almost, but it's a *lot* more complicated than that," he said in a tone that could be read as either understanding or condescending, depending on how she chose to take it. She wanted to lean toward understanding, but as he launched into another round of explanations, she started leaning toward the latter instead. The more he kept talking, the more certain she was that she'd been right—he just didn't want it to sound that simple. She kept waiting for him to ask her a question about herself, literally *any* question, but it obviously wasn't going to happen.

"Did you like her?" he asked, and she realized guiltily that she'd been running through a case she'd had during her last shift, wondering if she should have asked the patient, an elderly woman with a worryingly persistent cough, a few more questions rather than just ordering tests and sending her on her way.

"Sorry, you lost me," she said, and his indulgent smile said he wasn't surprised she was confused, and yeah, this date was going nowhere, fast.

"My assistant."

"Your—assistant?"

"Jenna."

"I don't know if I've met Jenna?"

"G-E-N-A," he spelled. "My chatbot."

"Oh, uh—"

"It's who you've been chatting with," he explained, and she immediately started rehearsing her exit strategy. *Oh, I'm sorry, I'm getting a call about a patient. This might be a while.*

"It wasn't you?" she asked innocently. Now some of the odder moments of their chats were starting to make sense—moments she had written off as the stilted interactions that came from boilerplate getting-to-know-you conversations.

"Don't worry, I reviewed it all before coming, so I know all about you. Gena is a side project, and I'm thinking I'll try and launch her in the next fiscal year. Dating is such a hassle; it's easier to outsource it, you know? I just put in all my personal details and a few anecdotes and she does the work of screening people out."

"Like a program that scans résumés."

Anders grinned. "Exactly! I'm glad you get it."

Oh, she got it all right. Daphne flipped her phone over, careful to keep the screen pointed away from him, and pulled an exaggerated apologetic face. "Shit, sorry, this is the hospital." She stood and walked away, pretending to answer. From her vantage point in the corner of the shop, she watched him pull out his phone and skim through something. *Probably another sucker talking to a computer program instead of him.*

She returned, hoping she appeared suitably apologetic. "I'm so sorry, but I have to get back to one of my patients. You understand how it is."

"Totally," he said, barely glancing up. "We should do this again sometime. Gena calculated our compatibility at a seven out of ten, so it's worth a shot, right?"

"Um—things are really busy, but maybe," she said, grabbing her purse. "Nice to meet you, Anders," she said, and hurried out of the coffee shop like her hair was on fire.

◆ ◆ ◆

Daphne walked into Ellie's room and flopped down on the bed. Brittany was there too, watching videos on Ellie's laptop while they lounged on her dark-red bedspread. They were a pair of contrasts, Ellie short with curly blond hair and Brittany tall and brunette with thick, dark-rimmed glasses, but both had generous curves compared to Daphne's narrow frame.

"That bad, huh?" Ellie asked.

"It was a chatbot," Daphne whined, face pressed into the mattress.

"A what?" Brittany asked.

Daphne lifted her head. "A chatbot. Who I was talking to, this whole time. It was a chatbot he'd set up."

Ellie sat forward. "No."

"Yes."

Brittany looked horrified. "Is that why he repeated himself so often?"

"I'm guessing. But don't worry, he reviewed the messages before our date."

"Wow," they said simultaneously.

"Yeah." Daphne dropped her face back down. "You were right, El—dating is stupid."

Ellie sighed. "It is, but I meant, you know, for me. You want that, so you should have it."

"How, though? Literally, how the hell am I supposed to find someone to date if I spend all my time at the hospital, and the only guys willing to talk to me on dating apps don't even bother to do the talking themselves?"

"I'm a bad person to ask that, seeing as I just do the fuck-buddy thing," Ellie replied.

"And I'm willing to date someone of literally any gender and still don't have time to actually take someone out," Brittany added. "It's the job, not you."

Daphne sighed and turned her head to look at them. "It still feels like there's something wrong with me."

"Of course there isn't. You're funny and smart and you look like a goddamn supermodel. If this guy wasn't into that, then fuck him. But don't *actually* fuck him, you know?" Ellie said fiercely.

This was well-worn territory for them. Daphne didn't agree with Ellie's assessment—after all, if she were as pretty as El claimed, wouldn't men be at least trying to date her? The handful of attempts she'd made over the years had always ended poorly, which just reinforced her *dating is a distraction* motto. And now that she was finally *ready* to date, she was apparently not even worth a real conversation first. "What good is being hot if I can only make small talk about the worst broken bones I've ever seen?"

"Please tell me you told Tech Bro Dickbag a gross story," Brittany said.

"I should have. Instead, I just lied and said there was an emergency with a patient."

"And he bought that?"

"I don't think he read enough of my texts with his chatbot to realize ED doctors wouldn't be following up with a patient like that."

Ellie patted the top of her head sympathetically. "He's not worth it."

"I know, I just—I thought maybe we'd click, you know? And then I'd have it."

"Define *it*."

"A life. *The* life, you know? I've always had a plan, and I figured I'd find a guy eventually, but now—it feels too late."

Brittany and Ellie exchanged a concerned look, and Ellie shook her head. "I swear to god, if you say you are too old at *twenty-seven*, I am going to kill you."

"It's not that. I know I'm not too old, but I still think I might be too late. Everyone else has at least a decade of practice with dating and relationships, and meanwhile I've had like, five one-night stands."

Ellie frowned thoughtfully. "That's not true. There was that guy sophomore year. What was his name?"

"Chris. He counts for three of them." Chris had been a nice enough guy in her genetics class, but she hardly considered hooking up after studying to really count as a relationship. He had gone abroad for their entire junior year, and by the time he came back, she was far too busy applying to med school to start anything up.

"Still, that's experience."

"Be real, El."

"Stop being so hard on yourself, Daph," Ellie replied in the same tone as Daphne. "But seriously, what do you want, exactly? In a guy, I mean—I know the rest of the whole life plan."

Daphne rolled to her back and stared up at the crack in the ceiling. She didn't love the idea of admitting it in front of Brittany, who was basically a stranger compared to Ellie. But residency had a way of trauma bonding people, and anyway—fuck it. She was in a mood lately, like something needed to change, so maybe it was her.

"Someone who cares. Like, cares enough to listen to gross hospital stories, even if he hates them. Someone who wants to spend time with me, even if I'm exhausted and cranky. Just someone I can hang out with, be myself around." She chewed her lower lip, thinking. "And honestly? I want romance. Real romance, not awkward small talk in a coffee shop. Or at least, not *just* awkward small talk in a coffee shop. I know you hate this shit, but I want, god, I don't know, candlelit dinners and love letters? Stuff like that. Someone who gives me butterflies, but who also makes me feel safe and wanted."

"You want to be in love," Brittany said softly.

"I know, it's pathetic."

"No, it's you. And it's out there for you, I know it is," Ellie said. "But in the meantime, I think I made you promise to do something stupid and impulsive next time we were both free, and today counts, so what do you say?"

Daphne lifted her head and made herself smile at her friends, because they were working hard to make her not so depressed. "I say, what did you have in mind?"

Chapter Three

Several days later, Daphne blinked against the bright sunlight, holding her hand up in front of her eyes. Despite the fluorescent lights of the ED, she always felt like she was emerging from a cave after a shift. She was bone tired and thought about just abandoning her bike on the rack for the day, calling a RideShare, and going straight home to collapse into her nice, big, soft bed, but the air was warm and sweet, and a lone bird chirped from its nest above the ambulance bay.

It had been a long, grey winter, and the thought of missing out on one of the first real spring days convinced her she had been right to ride her bike to work that morning, as cold and dark as it had been. Later, Daphne would wonder whether there had been some sort of mystical force at play, but for the moment, it simply felt like the right thing to do. Like the spring weather was calling to her.

Daphne rode down the street, past the buses belching fumes and the restaurants tentatively opening their patios for happy hour. The few people standing around outside were huddled in the small patches of spring sunshine, since the shade still held winter's bite. All she had on was the hoodie she'd thrown into her locker that morning and her scrubs, but as long as she stayed on the sunny side of the street, it wasn't too bad. The moon, looking lost in the daytime sky, slipped out from behind a skyscraper.

Half a mile later, she turned into a small park nestled in the heart of downtown. She rolled to a stop, breathing deep. Spring was still hesitant, a hint of green grass here, a budding tree there, but the air felt new and fresh, like anything was possible.

Again, in retrospect, there were signs. But for the moment, Daphne stood in the park and listened to the traffic trundling by, eyes closed and face lifted to the sun. It felt good, healing. What she needed to heal from, she couldn't say. Anders (or more likely, his chatbot) had tried to text her a few times, but after her complete lack of response, he'd stopped trying. It didn't hurt—he sucked—but she did vaguely wish there were a man out there who'd be willing to fight for her. Or at least not give up that easily. Another bird chirped, and Daphne inhaled the scent of new grass and soil warming in the sun.

She got back on the bike, aiming it for the side street that would eventually lead to the apartment complex all the residents wound up renting in, since it was not horrifically expensive and boasted only a short commute to the hospital. The road had a slight decline, just enough that she could start gathering speed and coasting, wind whipping through her hair as a few straight blond locks slipped free from her helmet. This time of day the street was quiet, just a few blocks from the towering buildings of downtown, lined by low, squat apartment buildings with dark-brown brick facades. She savored the feeling of freedom and let the wind blow away her doubts.

Up ahead, there was an odd shimmer to the air, almost like a heat mirage. Except it was only in the bike lane and reached up vertically, rather than horizontally. Besides, while the sun was warm, it was only early-spring-in-Minnesota warm, not nearly strong enough to heat the pavement enough for a mirage. Daphne squinted, and the shimmer twisted in the air like a tornado, darkening into a plume of smoke before winking out of existence entirely.

And then she blinked. Because it wasn't possible. One second, she was looking at the odd trick of the light in the empty street a few yards away, and the next, a man stood right where it had been. Just—standing there, having appeared out of thin air, like the mirage had simply deposited him right in front of her. He hadn't gotten out of a car and walked over, hadn't been on the sidewalk before—nothing. He simply wasn't there, and then he was.

Daphne stared at him, bewildered, and he stared back. It was so odd, so distracting, that she didn't realize exactly where he was standing until it was too late.

And then she ran straight into him.

Daphne hit the ground, bike tangling with the man she'd just hit. She let out a loud *oof* and rolled clear, gasping for air. She took a beat and assessed herself—she hadn't hit her head, and there weren't any broken bones as far as she could tell, either. She had a large scrape up the side of her calf and she'd banged her elbow pretty badly, but neither was something some disinfectant and bandages couldn't handle.

She turned to the man she'd hit. "Are you okay?" she asked. "I'm sorry, I didn't see you there." He didn't reply, which wasn't a good sign, but maybe he was just dazed. He was looking around, eyes wild, like he'd never seen a city street before. "I said, are you okay?" she repeated.

Finally, he looked at her. His eyes were blue, she realized, completely unnecessarily, but then she realized he was staring at her like she was an animal in the zoo. "I—my God, what are you wearing?" he asked in an accent she couldn't quite place.

Up close, Daphne could see that he was dressed oddly formally for a Thursday afternoon—a three-piece suit, it looked like, although there was something slightly off about it. The fabric was too thick, and the tie seemed strangely old-fashioned. A costume, she decided, although for what she couldn't say. And he had been wearing a hat—not a winter hat, or a baseball hat, but an Abraham Lincoln–type hat. That was now a good three feet away, knocked clear by the force of their impact.

"I could say the same to you," Daphne replied dryly. She pushed herself up, dusted herself off—her scrubs were shot, but she had more—and knelt next to him. No blood, no visible trauma, at least. "I'm a doctor. Did you hit your head when we crashed?"

He cringed away from her, glancing desperately up and down the street, as if he were looking for rescue. "Miss, I—whatever it is you think you are doing, I must insist you stop."

Daphne kept her eye roll in check. She'd had difficult patients before, and someone being a jerk didn't make her not a doctor. She just had to retreat into what she and the other residents called their Doctorsona, otherwise known as "pretending the mean shit a patient just said doesn't bother you."

"Please let me check you out. You may have a head injury," she said, just a touch more coolly.

His face still contorted in shock, he looked at her bike, which was badly mangled and half on the street, half up on the curb. "Is that a *bicycle*?"

Make that definitely a head injury. He scooted away from her again, once more eyeing her suspiciously. He had a pocket watch, she noticed, and she decided he was either a lost cosplayer or an actor on his way to rehearsal. Or maybe just a very, very weird person. He started looking around again, vaguely terrified. "Miss, where—where *are* we?"

And there's another bad sign. Shit. The last thing she needed was to have given someone a traumatic brain injury. "Minneapolis."

If she'd thought that information would calm him down, she was wrong. "The mill town? In *America*?"

She wouldn't call it a mill town, although downtown had that GOLD MEDAL FLOUR sign, and there was definitely a museum nearby called Mill City or something like that, so it probably had been, at some point. But she decided to sidestep the issue entirely, because honestly, that was a weird way to describe a major metropolis. "We're in the United States of America, yes. I'm going to check your pulse and do some simple tests, okay? As I said before, I'm a doctor."

"Nurse," he said, without really looking at her. "You mean you're a nurse."

Oh good, he's one of those. "Doctor," she repeated.

He sighed, aggravated. "If you were a woman doctor, I would have read about you in the newspapers," he insisted. "Maybe it's you who has the head injury."

Daphne decided to ignore his accusation and took his wrist in her hand. "If you didn't think you were in Minneapolis, where do you think we are?"

He looked around, jerking his arm away. She wasn't that worried about his pulse, all things considered, but procedures were procedures. "Edinburgh?" he said, and this time when he spoke, she picked up his accent. He was, unfortunately, off on the location by several thousand miles, but maybe he was just a tourist who was concussed. Hopefully.

"What day is it?"

"Thursday."

"Correct." That was encouraging, at least. "And what year is it?"

He looked at her strangely again. His dark hair was mussed, and there was just a tint of red to it, being picked out by the sunlight. He was handsome, she noted irrelevantly, and then he spoke, and she forgot his looks entirely. "Miss, if you don't know what year it is, perhaps *you* need to see a doctor."

"And why is that?"

"Because it's 1885."

Chapter Four

"I'm sorry, did you say 1985?"

He looked at her like she had grown an extra head. "*Nineteen* eighty-five? No, I said *eighteen* eighty-five."

Surprise made Daphne temporarily forget her Doctorsona. "Like, olden times?"

That extra head of hers was still there, judging by how he stared back. "Whatever does that mean? Are you quite all right, miss?"

"I told you, I'm fine. It means, um—" She stopped, not sure whether she should embrace whatever delusion the TBI was causing. "Just to be clear, to you it's 1885?"

"Is it *not*?"

Okay then. Back to the hospital it is, Daphne thought. Out loud, she put on her brightest voice. "If you can stand up on your own, I can help you to the hospital." She grabbed her bike—the wheel was bent, and it would need a tune-up, but it could be salvaged.

He frowned and stood, no apparent injuries other than a small scrape on the edge of his jaw, and picked up his hat. Another glance around at the buildings had him looking even more puzzled, and then he put the damn hat on and looked both puzzled *and* weird. "Is this truly what America is like?" he asked.

"Uh, yes? Don't you have, um, buildings in Edinburgh?"

He sent her an unmistakably annoyed look. "Yes, we have buildings. But not—like this."

Since Daphne had no idea what the city skyline of Edinburgh looked like, she couldn't exactly refute that. "Are you visiting?" she asked, deciding to try and suss out just how deep his confusion went, even though that *women aren't doctors* thing still bothered her, concussion or no. Hitting one's head didn't tend to turn a person into a misogynist—that tended to be there all along. Then again, he also claimed to be from the 1800s, so maybe the problem was a lot bigger than a bonk on the head.

"Don't be ridiculous. How could I be visiting?"

"So you live here?"

He sighed. "As I said, miss—"

"Doctor. Dr. Daphne Griffin," she corrected, but he skipped right over her interruption.

"I live in Edinburgh. However I got to wherever we are, I couldn't say." He spun around on his heel. "Did you bring me here?"

"*Bring* you? I've never met you. How could I have brought you here?"

Clearly, he didn't believe her. "Miss, I insist. Undo it."

"Undo hitting you with my bike? I'd love to, but that's not possible."

"Then explain how I could be in Edinburgh one minute, and in *America* the next."

"You hit your head. You've probably got a concussion." Although she couldn't remember ever seeing or hearing of a case where a concussion made someone think they were from a different century. Usually that sort of delusion meant there was serious mental illness, brain trauma—like, the type you could see—or a tumor. *Oh god, he's got a tumor.* Hitting a man with her bike and immediately telling him he had brain cancer would be a *really* shit way to end the day. Worse for him, obviously, but still, not great for Daphne, either.

"Nevertheless, I must return home. My mother and sisters will be waiting for me."

"Please, um, sir," she said, deciding that if she went along with his way of speaking, maybe he'd listen to her. "The hospital is this way. We can locate your family once you're there." She motioned for him to follow her, and he did, albeit hesitantly. She walked her bike, the spokes ticking softly.

He kept stealing glances at her, his face turning a little bit redder each time.

The third time he looked at her and then immediately looked away, she snapped. "What's the matter? Is there something wrong with me?"

If possible, he turned even more red, but he also refused to meet her eyes. "Miss, I—it's simply that you're wearing—would you mind? Covering up?" He gestured at her, and she looked down at herself.

Sure, her scrubs were a little ratty now, thanks to the spill she'd taken, and her hoodie had seen better days even before she ran into someone on her bike, but it wasn't like she was naked. "Covering up?"

"You cannot be so dense. What you're wearing? In public? It's positively indecent. We haven't even been introduced properly. Although with how familiar you're being, with no chaperone, perhaps I shouldn't be surprised."

Indecent? Oh no, she was definitely ditching this asshole with the triage nurse, whoever that happened to be at the moment. "Yeah, well, that's because I ran you over with my bike," she said dryly. "And I did just tell you my name."

"Yes, I am well aware of your claim to be a *doctor*."

Daphne stopped. "What the *hell* is your deal?"

"Oh good, you're foulmouthed in addition to being completely undressed in public."

"These scrubs are what I have to wear to work because I am a *doctor*, so I don't know what you expect me to do." Daphne wasn't sure why she was bothering, but bothering she was.

"For what purpose could you possibly be required to wear your *bloomers* in public?"

"Bloomers? The fuck are bloomers?"

That made him whirl around to face her. "With language like that, I'm starting to think you might not be a lady at all."

"I'm not. I'm a doctor."

He sighed. "That's simply not possible."

"Why? Because my brain is too small? My hormones will get in the way?"

"No. Because most medical colleges do not allow women to graduate. I know that for a fact."

"You do, do you?"

"Yes. Or else my sister Anne would be attending the medical college in Edinburgh now, if they allowed women to do more than merely observe."

It was official. This was the weirdest damn brain injury she had ever witnessed. Or maybe it was a longer-standing delusion—after all, thinking it was 1885 would explain his clothes. And the hat, which he was wearing like it was normal to cosplay as Abraham Goddamn Lincoln. But Daphne had encountered a lot of patients dealing with pretty serious mental illnesses, and they didn't usually present so rationally. He didn't have the typical signs he was struggling to hold on to reality. His thoughts were coherent and consistent, except for the part where he thought it was nearly a hundred and fifty years ago. Even tumors usually had other symptoms. The only other option was that he was extremely, extremely committed to a very weird, very annoying prank. She was honestly hoping for the tumor, as bad as it would be, because the other option was ending up on TikTok or some shit, thanks to some dude who wanted to go viral.

"Med schools have accepted women for a long-ass time," she replied. "It's the goddamn twenty-first century, after all."

Daphne had gone another ten feet before she realized he'd stopped walking. "What did you just say?" he asked.

"The twenty-first century."

"That's quite simply impossible."

"Oh, is it?" she said, far more sarcastically than her Doctorsona would, since by now her Doctorsona was hanging on by a thread.

"If it were true, that would mean I had traveled through time. And we may live in an age of astonishing progress, but time travel? That's preposterous."

To be fair, at no point had Daphne considered *that* possibility. "The other option is that you hit your head very, very hard, and now are confused about what year it is, and when you're from." *Very confused, and with clothes that match your delusion, which is also very strange,* she added mentally.

"I repeat, that's impossible. I recognize you might not be educated on the rules of physics, but—"

"For fuck's sake, *I am a doctor.*"

"Also impossible," he replied haughtily. "Not to mention, incredibly crude."

"Okay, you know what? Fine. Hospital's that way. You can go or not—I don't care."

"Charming," he muttered, but Daphne ignored him, deciding she'd take the light-rail back to her apartment.

A car breezed past, and she looked at him just in time to see him startle and jump several feet back. Whatever bit this was, he was *incredibly* committed to it. And the bit was oddly realistic, although her historical knowledge was mostly limited to a handful of romance novels and the Keira Knightley *Pride and Prejudice*.

She watched him stumble backward and trip over a small stand that held free local neighborhood flyers. Daphne snorted to herself when he fell on his ass. *Serves him right,* she thought, and turned away with just the smallest pang of guilt. She'd taken an oath to help, after all, but then again, she couldn't force someone to seek treatment, and if he wanted to keep pretending he was from a different century, there wasn't much she could do.

"Miss?"

Daphne kept walking, annoyed, until he called "Miss" again. Reluctantly she stopped. "Yes?"

"What is this?" he asked, holding out the small local free paper that always showed up in their mailbox and went straight into the recycling with the junk mail. He'd gone a little pale, and that *you took an oath* voice got a little louder.

"A newspaper. Don't you have newspapers wherever you're from?"

He shot her a dirty look. "Of course I know it's a newspaper. I meant—what is the meaning of *this*?"

"The date?" she asked, looking where he pointed. "It tells you the day, date, month, and year. I guess you don't have that back in 1885, then?"

He ignored her, a little more blood draining from his face. "Does it say—does it say the same thing to you?" Daphne confirmed it did, and then worried he might faint dead away as his complexion went grey. "Is this some sort of joke?"

"Why would it be? That's yesterday's date," Daphne replied.

"You're *sure*?"

"Of course I am. I know what year it is, and I promise, it is *not* 1885."

All the remaining blood left his face. He bent over, hands on his knees. *You took an OATH, dammit,* her conscience shouted, and she gave in. "Do you feel lightheaded?" she asked. He might be weird and rude, but she was a doctor before anything else. "Take some deep breaths. There you go."

"I keep hoping I'm dreaming. But I'm not, am I?" he said, half to himself. He looked up at her, clearly freaked out. His shockingly blue eyes pleaded with her to assure him it wasn't true.

She studied him closely, trying to figure out what the *hell* was happening, but until she got him a CT, there wasn't much she could do. "No, you're not dreaming," she said, as kindly as she could manage, given how annoying he was. "But like I said, I'm a doctor. A *doctor*, not a nurse, and I think there's a chance you have a traumatic brain injury from our crash. If you can keep walking, we're almost to the hospital, where we can treat you."

"Do I have another choice?"

"I can't force you. If you'd rather make your way on your own, you can."

He looked around again. "It's really the twenty-first century? Not the nineteenth?"

"It is."

"You're sure?"

"Absolutely."

He inhaled sharply and straightened. "Then I guess I haven't any other options. After you, my lady."

◆ ◆ ◆

James was at the triage station when she walked in, Mr. Time-Traveler-Traumatic-Brain-Injury lingering a few feet behind her, eyes wide. "You missed us that much, huh, Dr. Griffin?" James called.

"Bike accident," she explained, and held up her scraped elbow, just barely visible through the now-torn sleeve of her hoodie. "My injuries are superficial, but I think he's going to need some scans. He's a little confused."

James nodded. Honestly, the nurses handled far weirder things than the doctors did, and often bore the brunt of the way the emergency department was used as a substitute for actual mental health treatment. "Name?" he asked.

"Henry Frederick MacDonald," the man replied.

"Birth date?"

"January 5, 1856."

James paused. "Can you repeat that?"

"I suspect a TBI," Daphne interjected. "Like I said, there's been some confusion."

"She's referring to the fact that I'm from 1885," Henry said with surprising humor.

James, ever the professional, didn't raise an eyebrow. "That must be very confusing for you. Why don't we get you back to a room right now? If Dr. Griffin is willing, she can show you the way."

Honestly, Daphne had been planning on ditching him once he was through triage, but she felt a splinter of guilt. She'd crashed into him, and now he thought he was from an entirely different century, so the least she could do was hang out while he waited for a slot in CT to open up.

Daphne held the swinging doors open. "This way, Henry," she said, and he followed her, surprisingly obedient. His eyes bounced from side to side as he tried to take it all in, and whatever the hell she'd done to his brain—or whatever had been wrong in the first place—was pretty serious. The usual signs she would have looked for weren't present, since his speech was by all accounts coherent, if arrogant as hell, and his pupils were equal and reactive, but obviously something was majorly, majorly wrong. And not just with his personality.

She led him into a triage room, with wide glass doors that faced the main part of the ED, and pulled the internal curtain closed, holding up a hospital gown. "Change into this. You can leave your underwear on, and the tie—wait, do you *have* underwear?"

His eyes widened and he flushed again. "Why on earth are you even asking, my lady?"

"It's relevant. Are you wearing anything under your clothes?"

He swallowed and attempted to speak several times before managing it. He was really, truly shocked that she was asking about his underwear, it would seem. "I am wearing all the proper attire fitting a gentleman of my station, yes."

"Okay then. If it covers your whole body, take it off. If it just covers your genitals, then you can leave it on."

Henry looked about ready to faint. "Good heavens, the future is far more vulgar than I would have thought."

"Not my fault you're wearing something that looks like you belong in *Hamlet*. But anyway, tie goes in the back, and I'll come back in when you're done. If you need help let me know, and I'll find someone to help you," she instructed. He hesitated, and she sighed. Probably best to play along for now, until they could get him some treatment—or a bed up in

Psych. "Look, I know you probably have doubts about my competency, or whatever, but I promise, here in the twenty-first century, women are perfectly capable doctors."

He looked down at the flimsy gown with a frown. "It's not that. It's that I must protest that *Hamlet* jibe."

"Is that really what you need to do? Now?" Daphne asked, wrinkling her nose in annoyance.

"I'm a respectable businessman, not an actor."

"Understood. Now change."

He hesitated again. "This gown, it's—this is very thin. And you'll be back in? While I'm wearing . . . this?"

"Would it help you to know there's nothing I haven't seen?"

"Not particularly. That's actually quite intimidating," he said with that same flash of humor from earlier. "But I suppose I'll need to trust you, mustn't I?"

"Yep. Now change," she said, and stepped out to give him some privacy. After five minutes, she started contemplating asking if he needed help, but just when she decided to, the curtain swooshed open.

"Is this truly what people in hospital are required to wear, or is this some sort of elaborate joke?"

Daphne turned, and for the first time since she rode her bike straight into him, she got a good look at Henry MacDonald, erstwhile time traveler. He was tall, probably just over six feet, with his shins and calves bare and sprinkled with dark-brown hair. His hair was dark brown with hints of red, and curly in a messy, vaguely appealing sort of way. He was just ripped enough that she could tell through the shapeless blue gown, although not in Anders's *I spend all my free time at a gym* sort of way. She brought her eyes up to his face—a nice face, she had to admit, with a strong jaw and high cheekbones—and found him watching her with the tiniest smirk, like he knew what she was thinking.

"Why don't you lie down?" Daphne said authoritatively, to hide the way her ears were burning. "I'm going to start ordering some tests."

Henry did as she told him to, and for the next thirty minutes, he stayed patiently in the bed, following her instructions, even though just about everything bewildered him. The more she explained, the quieter he became. She was sort of relieved by that—he really was irritating—but also a little concerned. A spark in his eyes seemed to have gone out, which honestly seemed like a worse sign than his time-traveler story. She thought about asking if he wanted to watch TV, but given how deeply rooted the *I'm a nineteenth-century gentleman* fixation seemed to be, she figured that would probably give him an aneurysm, if he didn't have one already.

Despite his wariness, Henry sat through multiple blood draws and a round of X-rays, which at least confirmed he didn't have any broken bones. CT was backed up, as usual, and the results from the lab wouldn't be ready for more than an hour, which meant waiting. He had some scrapes that should be seen to, but she didn't want to start on that only to get interrupted by Radiology. And Daphne didn't like how quiet Henry had gotten. In a doctor-assessing-a-patient way, not that she *wanted* to talk to him. But they had a little time to kill, and they could either talk or sit in increasingly louder silence.

"Do you have any family, Henry?"

"Why? What sort of 'test' would require my family's presence? Will you be needing their blood as well?"

"I'm just making conversation. If you'd rather sit here quietly, we can do that, too."

A long silence followed, long enough that Daphne decided he would rather sit quietly, but then he spoke. "I have a mother and two sisters. I—think. I did in my life in Edinburgh, at least."

"No father?" Daphne winced internally at her own bluntness. Usually, she was better with patients, but Henry had her off balance for about half a dozen reasons. Mostly because she'd decide he was the absolute worst, and then he'd go and make a quip that made her reconsider. And Daphne loathed uncertainty.

"He passed when I was eleven."

"Oh, uh—sorry."

"It was a long time ago," he said softly, and then smiled wryly. "A very long time ago, apparently."

That. There. He had no business being charming, while also being weird and irritating.

"What about friends? And what do you do? Like, your job?"

"I have a friend named George, who has been like a brother to me since school. And I own an import firm. MacDonald's Imports."

Daphne snorted quietly. "Any chance you import ground beef and buns?"

He frowned. "We do some foodstuffs, yes, but not meat. Is there a reason?"

"Sorry, it's a joke. There's a popular, um, restaurant here with a similar name, that's all."

"Ah," he replied, and the resulting silence was at least a little less awkward and deafening than the ones that had preceded it. "And pardon me, but given all—this," he said, waving his hand toward the monitors next to the bed, "am I really to believe you don't have a way to get me home?"

"We could get you to Edinburgh."

Henry sat up. "Why didn't you say so? We need to go, immediately. Like I said, my mother and sisters—"

"We need to make sure you're healthy first," Daphne interrupted. *And also, who the hell knows if you really do have a mom and sisters.*

"Then as soon as we're finished, I must insist you take me home. To my time. Not to whatever version of Edinburgh you have now."

"That's not possible."

"Why not?"

Because once we figure out what's wrong with you, hopefully you'll realize you're not from nineteenth-century Scotland. Saying that felt too dismissive, but she also didn't want to give him false hope. "Um, because time travel isn't a thing?"

"You have the ability to take photographs of my bones."

"X-rays are really different from time travel, I promise."

"You truly can't get me back?"

"Truly."

Henry fell silent, fiddling with the blanket over his lap. "What about you? Do you have a family?"

"A mom and a dad, and a younger brother."

"Are your parents happy with your choice of profession?"

She didn't love the little italics he seemed to work into his inflection on *profession*, but she answered anyway, since at least now he wasn't begging her to invent a time machine. "They're thrilled, yeah. Really, really proud."

Henry gazed at her with an expression she couldn't read, almost like he was considering another question, but then the certified nursing assistant from Radiology showed up to bring them up for his CT.

Daphne tried to explain to Henry what a CT was on the way there, but there was a reason she hadn't gone into education, and that was mostly her inability to describe medical procedures to someone with absolutely zero context for modern medicine and an apparently inherent talent for getting on her nerves. By the time they reached the CT room, she was so annoyed she didn't even care that he looked freaked out by the machine. "Just lie down and let us take pictures of your brain," she snapped, exasperated. Constantly explaining *everything* was starting to grate on her.

Henry narrowed his eyes at her. "Pictures of my *brain*?"

"We're in the future, remember? Now. Lie. Down. And don't move, no matter what you hear."

"One would think a doctor might be a little kinder to their patient," he mumbled under his breath.

"Excuse me?"

"I said, one would think a doctor might be a little kinder to their patient," he repeated defiantly.

"I'm being plenty kind. Now lie down."

"You didn't say *please*," he replied, and Daphne was almost ready to screech in frustration when she noticed the gleam in his eye.

"Are you seriously fucking with me? Right now?"

He fought a valiant battle against a smile. "I can't say I'm certain what *fucking with you* means in this century, but I'll hazard a guess and say aye, I'm fucking with ye."

His Scottish burr came through stronger than usual on the last few words, and Daphne found herself also losing a fight with the corners of her mouth. "For Pete's sake, just get on the table, okay?"

From the booth behind them, Meghan, her favorite radiology tech, pressed the intercom. "You guys okay in there?"

Henry jumped half a foot and looked around for the source of the sound. "You lot have far too many ways of scaring a fellow, you know that?"

"We really don't have all day, Henry. Just—please, let's get on with it, okay?"

"All right," he agreed and gingerly lay down on the table. "But if something goes wrong, will you pull me out?"

He looked worried all of a sudden, more worried than even the blood pressure machine had made him. Against her better judgment, her heart softened just the tiniest bit. "I'll be right in there, watching," she said, and pointed to the booth. "You're safe, Henry, I promise."

"Thank you, my lady," he said, and she made a mental note to ask why he'd switched from *miss* to *my lady*, but they really didn't have time to expand on his reasoning. And besides, hopefully he'd be sent off to another unit soon, for treatment of some kind.

"I hear you ran him over because he thinks he's from *Bridgerton*," Meghan said as soon as the door to the booth clicked shut, leaving Daphne to wonder how that particular interpretation got started. She began the CT scan and glanced at Daphne. "Did he piss you off or something?"

"I did not run him over *on purpose*."

"Okay, but if you did, at least he's hot, right?"

"It's somewhat less attractive when a man thinks he's from a century where the idea of a woman doctor makes him faint. Which means he's got a brain tumor, a massive TBI, or else he's just a stone-cold weirdo."

"Which one are we rooting for?"

"Noncancerous tumor," Daphne replied. "Easily fixed with surgery."

"Hmm," Meghan said, squinting at the monitors in front of her as the images of Henry's brain appeared. "Not sure we'll have that luck."

Daphne wasn't a radiologist, but she could read a CT for basic major issues. And as far as she could tell, Henry had no hint of any sort of brain deformity, tumor, bleed, or anything else. It looked like a perfectly normal, healthy brain.

Which meant it was time for a psych consult.

Chapter Five

Daphne stood outside Henry's room, chewing on her fingernail and pacing. Ellie was on shift now, but Vibol and Brittany were off today, and if Michelle was working, she would be way up in Obstetrics with her patients, so Daphne would have to deal with this on her own. The psychologist on call was in there with him—and had been for nearly a half an hour. *Please just let him be admitted to the psych ward, please let him be admitted to the psych ward,* she prayed, although she wasn't sure who exactly she was praying to. Whatever deity was in charge of handsome men with pleasant accents and very strong delusions, maybe. She wanted to be able to wash her hands clean of Henry and get on with things. Daphne had a very full life, and she didn't have time to waste on some man who didn't know not to stand in the bike lane. She had to water the plants in their neighbor Helen's apartment while she was down in Florida and, well, other stuff. Like bingeing *Parks and Rec* for the fiftieth time.

Finally, the door opened, and the psychologist on call, Dean, came out. "What's the verdict?" she asked.

"I'll tell you what I told him: His thoughts are perfectly logical and coherent, and there's none of the usual disordered thinking that we would see with a delusion or hallucination. No ID on him, or phone, but he knows everything we'd want him to know about himself. He knows who he is, what his job is, and he's capable of making informed decisions."

"Except he thinks he's a time traveler."

"Except he thinks he's a time traveler," Dean agreed. "Which is a pretty big *except*."

"So you'll admit him?"

Dean looked sad and shook his head. "I could, if you want to do an involuntary hold, I guess, but we don't have any free beds, so he'd have to stay down here indefinitely until one opens up. And, well, he's otherwise perfectly sane. You said you didn't see evidence of a TBI? Or tumor?"

"Nothing. Still waiting on Radiology to confirm, but—maybe he's just very committed to the bit?"

"Possibly?" Dean agreed. "It's as good a guess as any, although I'd put my money on TBI. But I don't think Psych is the place for him. Sorry I couldn't be more helpful," he added, waving as he walked away.

Daphne swallowed hard and marched into Henry's room.

"The doctor said I'm perfectly sane," he announced. "Which is a relief, as I hadn't realized you thought I was mad."

"You think you're from"—Daphne screwed up her face and did some quick mental math—"about a century and a half ago. So yes, I thought you were 'mad.' And you still might be, honestly."

"Are mental hospitals as terrifying here as they are in my time?"

"I'm gonna go out on a limb and say no, although I can't say I know much about your time," Daphne said. "History was never my thing, you know?"

"Ah," he said quietly. "So, what shall you do with me?"

"Honestly, no idea. We're still waiting on some labs."

"And what will these 'labs' tell us?"

"They're the blood tests. They'll tell me if you have any markers for encephalitis, for example. Or any other diseases that could be causing this delu—belief."

"The other option could be I'm telling the truth," he countered.

"Yeah, well, I'm a woman of science. I'd rather it be a disease, quite frankly."

"Comforting," he muttered.

"Shut up and let me clean out that scrape on your jaw," Daphne sniped. That sort of thing usually fell to nurses, but they were already overloaded as usual, and it wasn't like Daphne was doing anything. And his scrape was minor enough that it probably didn't even *really* need attention. Which meant she was doing it for no apparent reason, but she'd already committed to it.

Daphne opened the drawer with the bandages and pulled out a bottle of disinfectant. "This will sting a little," she warned him.

Henry tipped his head to the side, giving her a good look at his admittedly nice profile. "Does it always sting, or are you just using that because I'm bothering you?"

"It's because you're annoying," she said. "Good patients get the non-hurty stuff."

"Pity I'm not a good patient, then."

"Stop talking so I can do this," she said, deciding that getting into banter mode with him was not a great plan. He fell silent, and she gently (but maybe not *that* gently) cleaned his cut and placed a bandage over it. "There. Should heal in a few days."

"Thank you," he said sincerely, and then frowned at her. "Your elbow—you haven't seen to it yet?"

"Oh, right," she said, flexing her arm. The skin felt tight, and she did need to *see to it*, as he put it. "Yeah, I probably should."

"Do you need assistance?"

"I can manage a bandage," she snapped, and then felt absurdly guilty when his face fell. "Sorry, it's been a long, weird day."

"I could say the same myself."

Daphne huffed out a laugh and pulled out another couple of bandages while Henry watched from the side of the bed.

"Are you quite sure you don't need help?"

"Quite," she replied. Daphne shrugged out of her hoodie—she would have to buy another, given how shredded the elbow was—and Henry turned away abruptly.

"I'll give you some privacy," he said stiffly. She vaguely remembered a romance novel she'd swiped from Ellie, where a man went into a complete meltdown over the sight of some lady's ankles. That would explain his freak-out over her scrubs too, and Daphne decided to cut him a tiny break and not tease him about it. She stood over the sink, hissing occasionally at the sting, and ripped the bandage open with her teeth. Not the most sanitary option, but fuck it. She was *tired.* She sank onto the stool in front of the computer station with a sigh, shrugging back into her ruined hoodie.

Her calf was a little easier to reach, and she didn't fail to notice that Henry glanced back at her and then immediately averted his eyes again when she hiked her scrubs up to her knee. She smothered a grin. "When exactly are you from?"

Henry looked at the floor. "1885," he murmured.

"Yeah, I know *that.* You've said that like, half a dozen times. I meant like, what's happening? Whenever you think you're from? Is it like . . . Shakespeare times?"

"Education in the modern world must be sorely lacking, if you think Shakespeare lived in 1885."

"Don't blame my teachers—I just never paid attention because it wouldn't ever be relevant for me. So I take it . . . no?"

"No," he sighed. "I am not from Shakespearean times, which would be approximately two hundred years ago. For me. Quite a bit further back for you," he added. "The queen is Victoria? Is there still a queen?"

"No, you guys have a king now. Definitely not Victoria, but that's also not that helpful for me. What sort of technology do you have?"

"Technology? The, uh . . . telephone is recently in vogue? Did that stand the test of time?"

"It did, and it's gonna end us all," Daphne said darkly, but a notification on the computer that his results were in from the lab saved her from having to explain social media to a man who already probably thought she was a witch or something. She would have to look up when witch-burning ended.

She skimmed through the results, chewing on the inside of her cheek. No encephalitis—all the counts were where they were supposed to be. Just like the CT: He was perfectly healthy, except for the big, glaring thing that said he wasn't.

Daphne scrolled down to the tests she'd ordered as a way of proving to him he *couldn't* be from 1885 and frowned to herself. "Did you grow up . . . in a cult? Or on a commune?"

"I was raised in my mother's home in Edinburgh, in the Church of Scotland. No cults."

"Okay, but like—you have the *weirdest* set of antibodies I've ever seen?"

"My . . . body is odd?"

"No, your—oh god, I can't explain it. You've been exposed to some weird shit, I mean."

"Such as?"

"Well, I mean, you haven't been exposed to stuff you should have been if you were vaccinated, like rubella and polio. We usually see that in people who grew up off the grid, or with parents who hate vaccines."

"I don't follow."

"I didn't think you would," Daphne admitted. "But you have measles antibodies, so you've had that?"

"When I was eight. Four children in my neighborhood died that winter."

"Oh. Sorry," Daphne said again, and Henry motioned for her to continue. "No chicken pox immunity either, and—" She stopped and read the final line of the report to herself four times. "Shit," she swore, and lurched off the rolling stool near the computer. She crossed the room in two strides and grabbed his arm, a stupid, irrelevant voice in her brain noting that it was *a very nice forearm, all things considered*, and scanned for any telltale bumps. The skin was smooth and unmarred, but she grabbed his face and tilted it toward the light, looking behind his ear, under his jaw, anywhere it might be hiding. She'd seen it only in pictures, but it wasn't exactly a subtle disease.

"Is there a reason you're mauling me?" he asked, and Daphne let him go, her heart still racing.

"You've been exposed to goddamn *smallpox*?" That had been her ace in the hole, the test that she was going to use to definitively prove to him he wasn't from the past. They'd stopped vaccinating for smallpox in the US sometime around when her parents had been born, and it was declared completely eradicated shortly after that. No one born in the last few decades of the twentieth century, or the entirety of the twenty-first, had ever been exposed. It was next to impossible for anyone under the age of fifty from anywhere in the world to have smallpox antibodies.

But Henry did.

"I don't have it, if that's what you mean." He straightened the collar of the hospital gown with as much dignity as someone in one of those could.

"But you've been exposed. Which is literally impossible, unless you've been vaccinated."

"You mean inoculated?" Henry asked conversationally. "Of course I have. You haven't? You have multiple machines that see inside our bodies, but you just let people die of smallpox? How cruel is this century?"

"No, we don't—we don't have smallpox anymore. No one does. It's gone. We eradicated it a long time ago. Wait, they had vaccines back then? In 1885?"

"Again, I'm assuming you mean inoculations, and yes, we have those. For smallpox, at least, although I gather from your tone you have others." Daphne pulled out her phone and did a quick search, and—holy shit, Britain had had mandatory smallpox vaccines starting in the 1840s.

Henry Frederick MacDonald was telling the truth.

He was actually, literally, truly, from the past.

Chapter Six

Daphne stared at Henry. "You're—you're really from 1885, aren't you?"

"Aye. And I'd like to get home. I assume there's a machine for that, too?"

"You mean a time machine? I already told you, those don't exist."

"I thought that was a ruse to make sure I completed my treatment here."

"Well, it wasn't."

His brow furrowed. "Then how did I get here?"

"Your guess is as good as mine." Daphne shrugged.

Henry opened his mouth again, but before he could ask anything else, Ellie breezed in. Her hair was tied back in a messy bun, and she had a white stain on the side of her scrubs. "I hear you hit someone with your bike?" she said without preamble. She looked at Henry and wrinkled her nose. "Must have been you, huh?"

"Henry, this is Dr. Ellie Levine. Ellie, this is Henry MacDonald."

Henry had jumped to his feet when Ellie came in, and he did a little half bow, half nod thing that made Ellie shoot Daphne a puzzled look. "You must be another lady doctor. Pleased to meet you," he said, absurdly formal.

"I'm Emergency Medicine, not OB-GYN," Ellie replied, confused.

"He means like, your gender. Not your specialty," Daphne clarified.

Ellie cocked her head to the side. "Oh. Uh, yeah, I'm a lady, so . . . yeah?"

Daphne peeked out the door to make sure no one else was on their way in. "El, I've got to tell you something. There's literally no other way to put this, but—god, this is so weird. Okay, here goes. He's a time traveler—"

"From 1885," Henry interjected.

"Yeah, then."

"Daph, James said you were fine, and the patient had, some, uh, possible issues, but—girl, do *you* need a CT?"

"I didn't hit my head. And I was wearing my helmet. I don't know how to explain it, but this is the truth. He showed up out of nowhere right before I hit him, and he's from the past. I have no idea how to prove that to anyone, except with this." She pulled up the test results and let Ellie sink onto the stool.

Ellie skimmed through the lab report the same way Daphne had, frowning at various points and nodding at others. And then— "Holy shit, he has smallpox," she hissed, shoving as far away from Henry as she could. She jumped up and started pacing. "We need to call—I don't know, the CDC? But we have to lock this room down right away. How the *fuck* did he get *smallpox*?"

Ellie's panic mirrored her own just a few moments earlier, but it helped ground Daphne. "He doesn't have it. He's been vaccinated against it."

Ellie stopped in her tracks. "What? They stopped that decades ago."

"They did. But if Henry's from 1885, smallpox vaccination was mandatory then."

"Daph—"

"Ellie, listen to me. I know this sounds absolutely bananapants, but—"

"Bananapants?" Henry interrupted. "What are banana—"

"It's a saying. Means *weird*," Daphne said, and turned back to Ellie. "Look, I know how it sounds, but if you've ever loved me, you have to trust me on this. I was riding my bike, and he just *appeared*. No cars nearby, no doorways he could have stepped out of, nothing. He wasn't there, and then he was, and he's been very consistent on his story—he's from Scotland in 1885, and given the evidence, I don't know what other conclusion we can reach."

"He could have grown up in a cult," Ellie argued.

"I didn't," Henry replied.

"Besides, how would he have been exposed to smallpox?" Daphne pointed out.

"I don't know, cults are fucking weird. There could be a smallpox cult out there."

"El, I get it. It's—not believable. But it's what happened, I swear."

Ellie sat back down on the stool. "He's a time traveler. Okay, sure, why the fuck not?" she muttered. "Now what? Where do we go from here?"

"You handled that remarkably well, Miss Levine," Henry said. "A little profanely, but well."

"Uh, thanks?"

"You're quite welcome."

"What do we do with him?" Ellie asked, turning to Daphne.

Daphne shrugged. "I had just finished processing the time travel thing myself when you came in. Psych said they don't have room for him, and anyway, he's perfectly sane, just—"

"From the past," Henry supplied.

"Exactly. So that leaves . . . the social worker?"

"So Kiana can send him to a shelter? Those are already overflowing, and if he's from, um, the past, then how is he going to manage literally anything?"

"Maybe an inpatient program of some kind?"

"You yourself just said he's not mentally ill," Ellie countered.

"Well, do you have any bright ideas? Or are you just going to shoot down mine?" Daphne grumbled.

Henry cleared his throat. "Would either of you two ladies consider asking me where I'd like to go?"

Daphne stifled an eye roll. "And where would you propose going? Time machine is still out, as we don't have that technology."

"And I still find that hard to believe."

"Believe it or don't—either way, you're stuck in the twenty-first century for now," Daphne said.

"Then I guess no, I don't have any ideas," Henry admitted, and sat back down.

Ellie rotated slowly back and forth on the stool. "I have an idea, but you're not going to like it."

"She won't, or I won't?" Henry asked.

"Daphne won't. She hates breaking rules of any kind."

"What are you thinking, El?"

"Helen's."

"No."

"Hear me out—"

"Who, or what, is Helen's?" Henry interrupted.

"Our neighbor. She's in Florida for the winter—wait, did you have Florida yet back then?"

"You mean the peninsula in the southern United States? Yes, that particular land formation existed."

"She meant if you knew of the state," Daphne said, not liking his condescending tone, seeing as Ellie was currently the closest thing he had to someone on his side.

"Again, I have some concerns about the state of education in this century."

"Blame Reagan," Ellie said with a hand wave. "Almost everything is his fault nowadays. Anyway, Helen's," she said firmly, and fixed Daphne with a look. "It's empty, and we know it will be empty for a while. It's just across the hall, so we could keep an eye on him, and we have the key. And there would be a locked door between him and us when we're sleeping."

"I object to the insinuation that you need protection from me. I am a gentleman, after all."

Daphne ignored him. "We promised Helen we would water her plants. This is not plant watering."

"She did say if we needed anything, we could help ourselves."

"I'm pretty sure she meant like, we could borrow a broom. Not store a whole-ass man from the nineteenth century in her apartment for god knows how long."

"Do you have a better idea?" Ellie asked.

Daphne sighed. "No. But what do we do in a month?"

"We hope we've sent him back home by then? Somehow?"

"I thought you said time machines don't exist," Henry said.

"They don't, but whatever brought you here has to go both ways, right? We just find whatever wormhole you slipped through and shove you right back where you came from. You know I'm right, Daph."

Daphne fixed Henry with a stern look. "If you steal anything from Helen, I don't care when you're from, I'll hunt you down."

Henry nodded seriously. "I wouldn't dream of it. You have my word, as a gentleman."

"Oh, well, if it's your word as a *gentleman*," Daphne snarked.

Now it was Ellie's turn to be defensive of Henry. "Jesus, Daph, don't be such a dick. He's really far from home, and it's gotta be scary as hell."

"Are all women in this century this prone to vulgarities?"

"Yes," Daphne and Ellie said together, and Daphne sighed. "Okay, so we discharge him, and we take him to Helen's. And then?"

"I dunno. We figure it out."

"How?"

"We're smart, and so are our friends." Ellie shrugged. "If we can all get into med school, we can probably fix this."

Henry nodded as if this were an acceptable plan. "If you'll kindly return my clothing, I can join you shortly at this Helen's."

"How are we getting home?" Ellie asked.

Daphne shrugged. "I was going to RideShare, but—light-rail? Wait, Henry, you know what a train is, right?"

He sighed. "Yes, I know what a train is."

"Okay, then we take that. Less freaky for you. We'll work your way up to being in a car."

"And what, pray tell, is a 'car'?"

"That thing that freaked you out and made you trip over the newspaper stand," Daphne explained.

"We'll explain later. Just get dressed, and we'll get going," Ellie said, and Daphne was relieved that—for the moment, at least—Ellie was in charge.

Because this was officially the weirdest day of her life.

Chapter Seven

"What are the odds we walk in there and he's like, broken everything?" Daphne asked as Ellie pulled out the key to Helen's the next morning.

Getting Henry settled had been quite the ordeal. He was freaked out by everything—the digital alarm clock, the microwave, the fridge—and that wasn't even touching on the fact that he thought she and Ellie might be sex workers when he discovered they lived on their own. It would have been nice to have Vibol around to manage Henry, but he'd already turned his phone to Do Not Disturb by the time they got back, and Ellie had pointed out that a disgruntled Vibol who got dragged out of bed to deal with a time traveler probably wouldn't have been very helpful.

"He's from the Victorian era; he's not a caveman," Ellie scolded.

Henry, who had been sitting on Helen's plaid couch, jumped to his feet. "My ladies," he said, tipping his head forward.

"How'd you sleep?" Ellie asked.

"Quite well. Twenty-first-century mattresses are spectacular." He followed them out into the hall and back to their apartment, still looking rather dazed.

"I sent an SOS to our friends, so they're coming over soon," Ellie explained. Daphne had hoped everyone would get there immediately, but Vibol had just woken up, Michelle was at the gym when Ellie texted 911, and Brittany was just leaving her hot paramedic crush's apartment, having finally succeeded in her monthlong flirtation campaign. They all lived in the same apartment building as Ellie and Daphne, though, so at least they'd all get there quickly.

"I got a text from Dean this morning, and he says you kidnapped a time traveler?" Vibol said, walking in without knocking. He stopped and looked at Henry, taking in his outfit—he had redressed himself in the suit from yesterday—with wide eyes. But his outgoing nature won out over his clear skepticism.

He held his hand out to Henry, who stood stiffly beside Daphne. "Vibol Law. Nice to meet you."

Henry shook his hand. "Henry MacDonald. Are you also a doctor?"

"Emergency Medicine, just like these ladies."

Henry shot Daphne a dry look. "You don't object when he calls you ladies?"

"It's different," Daphne gritted out.

"Vibol," Henry said, mulling over his name. "Are you from the French colonies in Indochina?"

Vibol pulled a face. "He really is from the nineteenth century, isn't he?" he said to Daphne. "It's, uh, not a colony anymore. And I'm from Massachusetts, but my parents are from Cambodia."

"Oh, my apologies. I've met a few sailors from your parents' part of the world. My business does a lot of trading."

Vibol nodded and leaned his hip against their countertop. "So what's the plan? How do we get Mr. Empire back to his time?"

"We didn't have much of a plan yet," Ellie admitted.

"Maybe we should ask Michelle?" Vibol said.

Michelle was an OB-GYN resident, and the smartest one of their whole group. Vibol also happened to have the world's biggest crush on her, a fact that everyone except Michelle knew.

"Why are we asking Michelle?" Brittany asked as she let herself in. "Vibol finally gonna do it and ask her out?"

"Shut up," Vibol grumbled.

Henry frowned. "Do you lot not lock your doors? Is that unnecessary in the future?"

Brittany stared at him. "The—future?"

"He's a time traveler," Vibol said cheerfully. He either had accepted Henry's story surprisingly quickly or had decided to believe it for maximum chaos. Either was plausible with him.

"A time traveler," she repeated dully.

"It's a long story," Daphne said.

Ellie opened a bag of tortilla chips and passed it to Vibol. "It's really not. Daph ran him over with her bike, and it turns out he's from the past."

Brittany looked at all of them suspiciously. "Are you fucking with me?"

"We're not," Daphne sighed.

Still frowning, Brittany stuck her hand out. "Dr. Brittany Spiers."

"Another lady doctor," Henry murmured. "Pleasure to meet you, Miss Spiers."

Brittany blinked. "Holy shit, he *is* a time traveler. He didn't do it."

"Do what?" Henry said, puzzled.

"There is not a single person alive today who could resist commenting on my name," Brittany said.

"There's something remarkable about it?"

"It's a pretty famous name," Vibol said from around a mouthful of chips. "Not knowing it means you're either *super* homeschooled or from the past."

"And you know I'm not this 'homeschooled' business how?"

"Too normal. I mean, you're not normal-normal, but homeschooled is a very particular vibe, which you don't really have."

"Ah," Henry said in a tone Daphne was rapidly coming to understand meant he did not, in fact, understand, but he was willing to let it go for the moment.

"What's this I hear about Daphne hitting a reenactor?" Michelle said as she walked in, tossing her long microbraids back over her shoulder. Vibol straightened almost imperceptibly. "The nurses on my shift were talking about it."

"Is this some sort of communal tenement flat?" Henry muttered.

"Not a reenactor, a time traveler," Ellie said.

Michelle stared at each of them in turn. "Um, what?"

"Henry's from the past," Brittany said.

"Have you all lost your goddamn minds?"

"Possibly," Daphne said. "But really, he is. He's been vaccinated against smallpox and everything."

"Well, Daphne doesn't have much of a sense of humor, so then it must be true." Michelle shrugged. "No offense."

"Definitely some taken, though," Daphne said, and Henry made a noise that might have been a laugh.

Michelle eyed him warily. "I assume we need to get him back?"

Ellie snatched the tortilla chips away from Vibol. "We do, but no idea how."

"Build a time machine?" Vibol offered.

"Do you know how to do that?" Brittany asked.

"No, I'm just here to be handsome and share good ideas." He preened.

Michelle rolled her eyes. "What about moons and signs and shit like that? If we can't science it, maybe we can, you know, woo-woo it."

"Woo-woo?" Henry asked, but no one answered his clear question.

"Don't look at me," Brittany said, adjusting her glasses. "I don't even know what sign I am."

"You're a Scorpio, and that is *such* a Scorpio thing to say." Ellie paused mid-chip as Brittany raised an eyebrow. "What? It's true."

"But do you know how it might work?" Daphne asked.

"Um, if knowing all your friends' signs gave me the ability to travel through time, do you really think I'd be here, with your dumb asses? No, I'd be off having a threesome with Paul Newman and Marlon Brando, like God clearly intended."

Brittany sighed. "James Dean. It was James Dean who supposedly had a threesome with Paul Newman and Eartha Kitt."

"My idea is pretty good too, though. You've got to admit it," Ellie said. Everyone kept looking at her, and she sighed. "But yes, I do know a lot about it, so let's see what we can figure out."

◆ ◆ ◆

"Any chance you like, pissed off a witch?" Brittany asked Henry, who was sitting at the kitchen counter, eating a piece of toast. (He had been very enamored with the efficiency of the toaster, not to mention the refrigerator, which he called "absolutely ingenious." His cautious, newfound enthusiasm for certain modern appliances was rather charming, Daphne had to admit, if only because he would probably yelp in fear a lot less if he found them exciting rather than terrifying.)

"How would one do that, Miss Spiers?"

"You can just call me Brittany."

"He really can't," Daphne replied. "Trust me."

Henry drained his orange juice—his third glass, as apparently this was a wildly luxurious drink in his time—and shook his head. "Miss Griffin is correct: Remembering the correct forms of address is challenging for me. But no, I have not 'pissed off a witch,' or at least if I did, I did so unwittingly."

"Okay, but like, do you have enemies? People who might hate you?" She stole a look at Daphne. "Jilted lovers, perhaps?"

"I have no paramours, and despite my mother's best efforts, neither am I engaged."

"Let's dig into that," Michelle said. "Were there women who wanted to be engaged and you turned them down? Maybe someone with an interest in the occult?"

"My mother had hoped to secure a betrothal with a woman whose father owns a railroad, believing that would aid our family business."

"And how did you feel about that?"

"I found Miss Mary to be a steady, companionable presence."

"That doesn't sound like you wanted to, um, you know," Michelle said, and Henry raised his eyebrows.

"She means it doesn't sound like you wanted to fuck her," Daphne translated.

Either Henry was getting used to her "vulgarities" or he was simply better at hiding his shock. "I did not," he confirmed. "However, it was she who opposed the marriage, as I believe she was—I'm not sure how to put this—not interested in the male species romantically?"

Brittany grinned widely. "Good for her. Anyone else?"

Henry hesitated, then shook his head. "No one who would bear me ill will, no." Daphne suspected that wasn't the whole truth, but she didn't think now was the time to push him on it.

While Michelle interrogated Henry on possible magical enemies, Vibol, Daphne, and Brittany were using a legal pad Michelle had retrieved from her apartment to make a detailed list of movies.

Research

- *Back to the Future* (no plutonium in 19th c)
- *Back to the Future II* (about future, not past)
- *Back to the Future III* (right year????)
- *The Time Traveler's Wife* (not a chronic illness unless onset was yesterday)
- *Inception* (dreams, not time travel)
- *Kate & Leopold* (Portal, maybe helpful?)
- *The Butterfly Effect* (Ashton)
- *Interstellar* (NO ONE UNDERSTANDS THIS ONE. NO. ONE.)
- *Everything Everywhere All at Once* (Not a multiverse???)
- *The Terminator* (No machines)
- *13 Going on 30* (was there a body swap? How can we figure it out?)
- *Bill & Ted* (brilliant but maybe not super applicable)
- *That Tom Cruise-Emily Blunt movie* (no one watched it)

"I still don't see how watching *Back to the Future Part III* is going to get him home," Daphne said.

"It won't, but we have to learn whatever we can about time travel, and unless you want to start reading super-dense philosophy and theoretical physics textbooks, this is probably the best way to figure it out," Brittany explained. "And I'm a nerd, but I don't really want to do that. Besides, we believe in science, and whatever happened here doesn't seem to be scientific."

"How do we know that for sure?" Daphne asked.

"Um, because time travel isn't real? Once you eliminate wrong answers, you have to go with whatever's left. Which is apparently magic."

"Are we sure it's not a multiverse? Shouldn't we put *Everything Everywhere All at Once* back on the list?" Vibol asked.

"You're just saying that because you're in love with Michelle Yeoh and want an excuse to watch her again," Michelle called from the other side of the room.

"Who wouldn't be?" he asked.

"So those are not books?" Henry asked.

"Movies. Plays, but you watch them on a screen," Ellie explained. She was sitting across the table, scrolling through astrology websites. "You said your birthday was January 5?" She was typing into her phone, face screwed up in thought. "What year again?"

"1856. How will this help?"

"It's a long shot, but I'll do your chart and see if that might have anything to do with it." At his blank look, Ellie hastened to explain. "Your star chart. You're a Capricorn, but knowing the rest of your whole chart might help if there's a supernatural element."

"And nothing like, brought you here, right?" Michelle asked. "No . . . ships?"

"As I said, I was walking, and I saw a shimmer in the air, and then I was here."

"I can confirm that," Daphne chimed in. "He just appeared out of thin air."

"Which means no time-travel device, got it," Vibol said, and crossed out *Bill & Ted* with a sad look on his face.

"Which means we're talking about a portal, not something man-made. Have we considered ley lines?" Ellie suggested.

"The hell are ley lines?" Brittany asked.

"Explain them to me like I'm five," Daphne asked.

"Magic places. Spots where there's a thinner veil between our world and supernatural forces. They crisscross the world, and some junctions are believed to have stronger powers than others."

"Wouldn't people be randomly time-traveling all the time, then?"

"For one thing, we don't know they're not," Ellie replied. "But there's probably a confluence of factors, like moon position, his star sign, that sort of thing. It'll take some research, though."

"How long might that take? I wouldn't want to impose upon your hospitality too long," Henry said. "Unless—would it be breaking some sort of twenty-first-century taboo if I stayed with Vibol?"

"No taboo, I just only have a studio. One room, that's it," Vibol said. "I'm a cuddler, but don't really want to spend however long sharing a bed with you, and I'm assuming you don't, either."

"I see. How long is the other flat open?"

"Helen's not back for over a month, so we've got time," Daphne said.

"I certainly hope it won't take that long."

"I'll go as fast as I can, but it'll take at least a few days, maybe a week?" Ellie was standing next to her, but Henry only made eye contact with Daphne.

"Then it seems you must put up with me for another week."

Chapter Eight

Slowly their friends trickled out the door. Vibol had a shift to get ready for, and Michelle had promised her uncle she would drop by that afternoon. Brittany's excuse was that she had to go back to her apartment and sleep since she hadn't gotten much the night before. Henry fortunately didn't seem to understand the implication there, at least.

But before they left, they had decided on a few things, mainly that Henry was obviously staying for at least a little while, so he needed to blend in better. That meant new clothes, but before Vibol would agree to loan Henry anything, he had to shower.

Ellie had taken the bull by the horns while Vibol went upstairs to get something that would fit Henry. They were approximately the same height, although Henry was somewhat broader in the shoulders. "Now you're going to take a shower," Ellie explained.

Henry looked befuddled. "A shower?"

"Yeah. You can use ours."

"We could wait on Vibol. He could teach him," Daphne suggested.

"First of all, Vibol has worse bedside manner than any of us, so no, he probably shouldn't be in charge of teaching a man from the past how to shower. Second of all, we're stealing the man's clothes and he has to get to work, so it's really up to us to teach him."

"Still waiting to learn what precisely you're supposed to teach me how to do."

"Take a bath. But standing up," Daphne said.

"I think I can manage that on my own."

"You really can't," Daphne retorted.

"I beg your pardon, I have been bathing myself—"

"Okay, I'm going to shut this down before you two work yourselves into a bickering frenzy," Ellie said. "Henry, I'll talk you through the basics, and Daphne will go buy you the rest of the clothes you'll need."

"The rest?" Daphne asked, raising her eyebrows.

"Well, I'm sure as hell not loaning him my underwear," Vibol said, walking back in. "Here's what I could find. Should work for a day or two. Good luck with"—he made a circular motion in the air at Henry—"all this. I'll check in on you guys when I'm off shift tomorrow."

Vibol shut the door behind him, and Daphne tried to get out of her assigned job. "He doesn't need underwear."

"He really does, though. And I have to go to the food pantry for my volunteer shift this afternoon, so we'd better get going. Henry, you know your measurements?"

"I do," he said, although the hint of a blush had shown up with the first mention of underwear and hadn't fully faded yet.

"Great, give them to Daph, and I'll talk you through the basics of plumbing. Daph, why don't you get him at least another outfit or two, since this isn't going to be fixed by tomorrow no matter what."

◆ ◆ ◆

Daphne got home half an hour later with a crinkly white-and-red plastic bag containing several pairs of pants, long-sleeved shirts, and the cheapest pack of boxer briefs she could find. She had googled "1885 men's underwear" while standing in the aisle, feeling like a pervert, and figured boxer briefs looked the most similar to what he was used to—assuming she hadn't stumbled onto like, fetish sites. At the last minute she'd grabbed him a hoodie too, since it was still chilly.

"He's been in there awhile," Ellie warned her. "I checked a few minutes ago, and he said he was fine, just 'marveling at the technological prowess' of our century."

"The hell does that mean?"

"I think it means he's impressed by unlimited hot water. Anyway, you'll have to convince him to get out eventually."

"How?"

"That's your problem; I already had to explain hot water heaters to him. I've gotta run, though. And Daph?"

"Yeah?"

"Be nice. He's not a dick, he's just really disoriented."

Daphne didn't feel like that was entirely fair, since she'd been perfectly pleasant to Henry most of the morning. But without the buffer of everyone else, she had felt her hackles rising even before she'd left on her errand, so maybe Ellie had a point. Daphne mentally chanted *be nice, be nice, be nice* as she approached the bathroom. She knocked but got no response. "Henry? It's Daphne. Are you okay?" she asked the door.

The water shut off, and she heard the curtain rings drag along the shower rod. "Henry?" she called again.

"What do you need, Miss Griffin?" he called.

"I have your clothes." She could feel his hesitation, and she sighed. "Remember, I am a medical professional."

"One moment," he replied, and she heard rustling before the doorknob twisted.

Daphne stepped back just as the door opened, and—well. Henry stood in the door with a towel tied around his waist, wisps of steam curling out from behind him. Apparently, they had gyms in 1885? Or weight lifting. Or else he was just very, very lucky in the genetics department, because his body was what she could only call *well formed.* Whereas Daphne had gotten the distinct impression that Anders waxed his chest, that was obviously not something men did in 1885, and Daphne suddenly had a newfound appreciation for history.

"Miss Griffin? Is anything amiss?" he said, and she jerked to attention.

"Sorry, uh—here," she said, and shoved the bag at him. "Clothes. You should be able to figure out how to get them on."

Henry emerged from the bathroom several minutes later, mercifully dressed. Daphne had chosen the clothes he was wearing, had seen him in a hospital gown, and had seen him in just a towel earlier, so she should have been prepared. She should have been, but she wasn't.

At. All.

It was a shame he lived in a time of three-piece suits, because he was born to wear a Henley. Those forearms were poetry worthy, honestly. His hair curled above his ears as it dried, and he eyed her warily.

Daphne couldn't blame him. It was easier for her with everyone else around, too.

Henry looked around expectantly. "Where are they?"

"They had to leave earlier, remember?" Daphne prompted. *Maybe he does have a major TBI, after all, if his short-term memory is this bad.*

"Not them." Henry sighed.

"Then who?"

"Your servants. I assumed, given the other dwelling was unoccupied, that they had traveled with their employer to her other estate, but you ladies must certainly employ some? A charwoman, perhaps?"

Daphne snorted. She had no idea what a charwoman was, maybe someone who . . . charbroiled things? That didn't seem like it would be a whole job, but maybe it used to be. "No, we don't have *servants*."

"I thought Ellie said you weren't poor?"

There was something about his haughty tone that irritated her, and she rolled her eyes. "No one has servants anymore unless you're like, royalty or some shit."

"Truly? Then how do things get done?"

"We do them ourselves, believe it or not."

"So you aren't ladies, then?"

This was easily the most annoying conversation she'd had with him yet, and that was saying something. "I honestly don't even know what that means."

Henry sighed, equally irritated with her. "Women of quality."

"You think having live-in servants is a sign of inherent morality? That we're beneath you? What sort of fucked-up time do you come from?"

"That's not what—"

"No, it is what you said. And look, I get that you're really freaked out, but that doesn't mean you get to insult my morals or whatever. I could have just left you on the street, you know."

"I know, my lady, but—"

"And that's another thing. Stop calling me *my lady*. If you want to be formal, you can call me Dr. Griffin, and if you can't bring yourself to address a woman as *doctor*, then just call me Daphne. But enough with this *my lady* shit, okay?"

He glared at her. "I do not mean to offend," he started.

"And yet you do, constantly," she grumbled.

Henry ignored her. "I cannot undo years of good breeding overnight, *my lady*. But I did not mean to impugn your character or manners. I simply meant where—when—I am from, people of higher social status, such as I believed you and your friends to be, have servants. As you do not, I was forced to assume that here, now, this must be poverty?"

"Jesus, no."

Another glare. His eyes flashed when he did that, and she felt an answering tug in her belly that didn't quite match her annoyance. "Then explain it to me, rather than sneering at my ignorance," he said.

Okay, that was fair enough. Daphne leashed her temper as best she could. "In the twenty-first century, we don't have servants. Almost no one does these days, aside from like, people with way, way too much money. Ellie and I make more than a lot of people, but nowhere near that much. We just do stuff ourselves, rather than have servants live with us."

"And do all women work, regardless of social standing? Or are you and your friends an anomaly?"

"Mostly, yeah. There's other reasons women don't, but it's not because it's like, improper or whatever."

"And are you . . . ladies? By your standards?"

"That's not a thing anymore. But we're perfectly moral, if that's what you're worried about."

"I wasn't. You have been very kind," he said, and then muttered something that sounded like *at least some of you* under his breath that she decided to magnanimously ignore. "Thank you for explaining that, my lady."

"I said—"

"And I said I can't undo years of habit overnight. In my time, calling you Daphne would imply an intimacy we haven't earned. For now, I implore you to let me keep that, at least."

His earnestness caught her off-guard. Daphne hadn't really considered *why* he kept calling her that, just that it bugged her. But she gave him a nod and pointed to the hoodie clutched in his left hand. "Is there something wrong with the sweatshirt?"

"Is that what this is? I must confess I found it baffling."

"What's confusing about it?"

"The mechanism." He held it up and pointed to the zipper. "How does this work?"

Daphne stared at him. "You don't know how a zipper works?"

He sighed, a sound that was rapidly becoming familiar to her. "For now, let's just assume that I do not understand anything about your world, yes?"

Daphne fought a losing battle with a grin. "You put it on like a jacket and then—I'll show you."

Henry shrugged into the hoodie and Daphne stepped closer, catching his scent, at once familiar and different. "You—here, is this okay?" she asked, motioning to the bottom of the zipper.

He made an affirmative noise and she hooked the two sides together, now acutely aware of how close they were standing. "You put this piece in here, and then just pull up," she explained, focusing a lot harder on zipping it up than was warranted.

She reached the middle of his sternum and stopped, glancing up. There was a ring of brown around his pupils, making the blue surrounding it all the brighter. Her mouth went dry and she licked her lips. "And there you go. Easy-peasy." *Easy-peasy? When the fuck have I ever said that?*

"Easy-peasy," he repeated, the corners of his eyes crinkling. "Is that a common saying here?"

Warning sirens sounded deep in the recesses of her brain, and Daphne stepped back, abruptly flustered. "Uh, yeah, uh, sometimes," she stammered, and decided that if she had to learn everything there was about astrology in the next week, she would. Because Henry needed to go home, stat.

Chapter Nine

Brittany stood in front of the TV with her back straight, hands clasped in front of her. "Henry, are you ready?"

Henry nodded from the couch, although he looked uncertain. "Will the images be moving?"

"Not these, no," Brittany said. "This is just a slideshow."

"And this will help me?"

"That's the plan," Daphne said from the armchair in the corner. She was curled up with a crossword puzzle (in ink, of course) while Brittany took the lead on their new group project.

"Then let's begin." Brittany turned the TV on to display the first image, which was a title slide.

GET HENRY ACCLIMATED TO THE 21ST CENTURY SO HE CAN STOP FREAKING OUT ALL THE TIME
BY BRITTANY SPIERS, MD

Henry had a notebook in his lap and looked for all the world like an earnest schoolboy, his arrogance for once set aside. Or maybe he was only like that with Daphne, since he seemed to challenge her more than anyone else.

The first slide was a picture of a crossover SUV, with the word *CAR* in all caps above it. "This is a car. It has an engine inside, and it runs on either gasoline or electricity," Brittany explained, sounding like a college professor even though her topic was "basic facts about contemporary life for someone who doesn't know anything."

Henry wrote something down, nodding. "How does the engine work?"

"No idea, but the gas version is very bad for the environment. And that brings me to my next topic: climate change." She advanced the slide using the clicker Ellie had bought for their New Year's Eve party, when everyone had been required to make a PowerPoint deck on the topic of their choice. (Vibol's topic of "My Favorite WWE Wrestlers" had been voted Most Unexpected, although they had all been pretty drunk by then.) "The planet is boiling, and we're all gonna die," Brittany continued. The image was of a factory belching smoke and a hazy sky. "We got addicted to oil back sometime around your time, and now we're fucked." She explained greenhouse gases and the burgeoning climate crisis while Henry's eyes got wider and he scribbled furiously. Next were planes ("please don't ask how they stay in the air—it mostly involves going really fast") and then phones, which caused Henry not a small amount of confusion.

"But a telephone is to talk to someone at the same time," Henry said. "You don't use them for that?"

"I mean, you can if it's absolutely necessary, but most of us don't."

"So you use them to send telegrams."

Brittany frowned at him, and after a bit of back and forth about what, exactly, a telegram was, she agreed, before diving into the topics of the internet and social media. Henry seemed delighted by the idea of the internet, although he struggled with social media—not because he found it self-absorbed, but because he couldn't understand why it made everyone so angry all the time. "Because that's what it's supposed to do," Brittany explained for the fifth time, before finally moving on.

Henry understood the idea of computers far better than Daphne would have thought, and he didn't seem to struggle with Brittany's slide on women (can vote and own property, don't have to have babies if they don't want to), and he was unexpectedly delighted by the idea of drag queens. "We'll take you to a drag queen brunch, then," Brittany said.

Henry wrote something down and looked up. "Is the next slide"—he checked his notebook—"brunch?"

Daphne snorted while working on eight down (*a walk, of sorts*), which she filled in with *stroll,* and Henry looked over at her. "What's amusing about that?"

"It's just funny, is all."

"Glad my ignorance can entertain you," he said haughtily, and Daphne looked up, ready to snap, but caught Brittany's warning glance. *He's really not that bad,* everyone kept insisting, and Daphne knew that was what Brittany was trying to tell her telepathically.

"It's not that," Daphne mumbled, and dived back into her crossword to avoid revealing the blush that was probably now staining her cheeks. Brittany explained she didn't have a slide about brunch because she hadn't expected to have to explain that it was just a combination of *breakfast* and *lunch*.

"And the drag queens bring you food?"

"Mostly they sing and dance," Brittany said. "But that's a good segue into my next topic: Britney Spears."

Henry grinned crookedly, and Daphne felt an absurd stab of jealousy. "I already know you fairly well, Miss Spiers."

"No, not me. My namesake." She advanced to the next slide, and now it was Henry's turn to blush, averting his eyes quickly from Britney Spears in her iconic schoolgirl outfit.

"She's, er, rather young?" he said, staring into his notebook like he hoped it would open up and swallow him whole.

"Yeah, she was sixteen or something when this was taken. This was her big break," Brittany explained.

"And what's the reason for, ah, her, well, her—"

"Her clothing? To make men want to have sex with her."

Henry's ears were bright red at this point, his eyes as wide as dinner plates. "And does that work? On men today?"

"I mean, it doesn't *not* work. But mostly I included her because that's how I knew you were telling the truth about being from the past. Even people living under a rock in the twenty-first century know who she is, because you can't not."

"And your parents named you after her? Does she have, er, remarkable qualities other than, er, well . . ." Henry stammered.

"Being hot? Yes, she's a good singer and a really great dancer. And I wasn't actually named after her. My parents just assumed she would be a one-hit wonder."

"What's a—"

"She means they thought she would have one song that got really popular, and then that's it," Daphne interjected.

"And that isn't what happened?"

Brittany sighed. "No, she's now like, one of the most iconic pop culture figures in the whole country."

"Do you mind being named after her?"

"I did, and I still do when people make a joke immediately after meeting me, like they're the first ones to ever make the connection between my name and hers. That's annoying as hell, but it's not Brit-Brit's fault, you know? She's just living her life and I'm living mine. She's got way more money, but my family is about 4,000 percent less fucked up, so I probably come out ahead in the end, jokes or no."

"Understood," Henry said seriously. "What's next?"

"Next up: men."

"We have those in the nineteenth century, too," Henry said dryly.

Daphne snorted again, but this time, Henry tossed her a grin. Her stomach felt oddly melty, and she redoubled her efforts to figure out the answer to fifty-one across (*ancient goddess, not Venus*). "What are you working on there, Miss Griffin?" Henry asked.

Daphne could recognize an olive branch when offered one, so she held up her newspaper. "Crossword puzzle." Henry cocked his head to the side quizzically. "It gives you clues, and then the answers fit together into one another." She read off the clue she was working on, and Henry frowned.

"Aphrodite, I would think," he suggested, and Daphne was half delighted, half irritated to discover he was right. Delighted because it had been a tough one for her, and irritated because Henry was not supposed to be kind and helpful, and also once he said it, the answer was so obvious she couldn't believe she hadn't figured it out on her own.

"Thanks," she muttered, and Henry turned back to Brittany, who was now showing him a stock image of a white man wearing a beanie in front of a podcasting microphone with a giant red *no* symbol encircling him.

Brittany walked him through the basics of twenty-first-century masculinity, while Henry nodded and frantically took notes. Daphne returned to her puzzle, lifting her head only when Henry started to sound angry.

"You have guns that do *what*?" he said. "What use could any civilian have for a gun that powerful? But you said people are allowed to simply *own* them?"

"Well, yeah, but only here in the United States. Pretty much everywhere else has way better laws about guns."

"What is wrong with your country?"

"That's the question," Brittany replied archly. "It sucks."

"It really does sound like a lot of the modern world, as you say, *sucks*."

"You're not wrong, but there's good stuff, too. Like for women, LGBT people, and people of color. You guys don't have much in the way of colonies anymore either, and that's good, too. And we can get places a lot faster."

"With—" Henry flipped back through his notebook. "Aeroplanes. And . . . cars?"

"Exactly," Brittany said.

"*Airplanes.* Not *aeroplanes*," Daphne clarified.

Brittany was the one who threw her a dirty look that time, shaking her head when Daphne responded with an innocent *who, me?* look in return.

"We're going to move on," Brittany said pointedly. "Ready, Henry?"

"Ready, Miss Spiers."

Chapter Ten

If Daphne thought Henry's high regard for manners would make him a slightly easier person to live with while they tried to figure out how to get him back in time, she was wrong.

Fortunately, she had sort of suspected he would be terrible. He was constantly questioning everything she did, down to whether it was safe for her and Ellie to live alone.

"Why? Because we might bring home a stray man who time-traveled from two centuries ago?" she asked to that one, thoroughly fed up.

"Well, yes."

"Should we kick you out, then? To preserve our virtue?"

"I was simply *saying* that I find it surprising that no male relative objected to your living situation."

"And as I've said, that's not a thing anymore."

"Still, they've severely neglected their duties. Vibol may be an excellent fellow, but there's four unmarried women in your group of friends, which is a lot of responsibility."

Daphne leaned her head back against the couch, reminding herself to breathe, even while trying not to laugh at the idea of Vibol thinking they were his *responsibility*. "Yes, I'll be sure to tell my younger brother he should have negotiated for someone to take my hand in marriage. Didn't you learn anything from Brittany's lesson the other day?"

"Assuming your father is alive, that would be his responsibility," Henry replied dryly. "And it's not that I didn't follow. I just don't see why it changed so drastically. Things worked fine as it was."

"Do you honestly think that the women in your life appreciate you making all the decisions for them?"

"It's my duty to look out for their welfare."

"That's not what I asked," Daphne countered. "Do your mom and sisters like that you run their lives?"

"They appreciate my concern. I handle worldly issues, while they're allowed to immerse themselves in the home."

"Okay, but you said one of your sisters would have wanted to be a doctor, right?"

"Anne has a sharp and inquisitive mind and an interest in healing, yes."

"But you wouldn't let her go to med school, even if she could?"

"It's irrelevant. She can't."

Daphne swallowed a screech. "Humor me. Pretend she could. Would she?"

"I would be concerned that it might be too much for her," Henry replied.

"That's not an answer."

Henry fixed her with a look. "You're going to argue with me about my answer."

"Meaning no, you wouldn't let her."

"Correct," he sighed, apparently giving in to the argument. "I would not allow her to go to medical school. There are things that, no matter how different your time is, I think are simply too difficult for women to handle. Not intellectually," he said, clearly foreseeing her next argument. "Simply that a woman is built for nurturing, not cutting people open."

"That's just offensive."

"I'm sorry, my lady. I am simply explaining the truth as I see it."

"For one thing, I don't care if it's the truth as you see it—you're wrong. Your mother and sisters might be *used* to you running their lives, but I promise you they don't enjoy it."

"I know them, however," Henry countered. "You have never met them."

"True, but I know *people*. And no one likes having their brother or son run their life, okay? They might be *used* to it, but I promise, if they had another option, they'd take it."

Henry looked at her, blinking. "You seem very certain."

"I am. I might not know a ton about history, but I do know that life for women was pretty shitty until relatively recently."

He sat quietly on the couch for a moment, the silence stretching long enough that she got uncomfortable. "What's wrong?"

"You've given me a lot to consider," Henry said.

"Okay, you know what? We should wash your other set of clothes," Daphne said, mostly to get herself out of the conversation. It was easier if Henry was deliberately being a misogynist, rather than simply not knowing any better. She didn't want him to *learn*; she wanted—well, she wasn't sure what she wanted. "And if you're going to be here, you should learn how to use the washing machine."

"You have a device that washes machines?"

Daphne glared at him, annoyed when she almost cracked a grin as he looked at her evenly. He was fucking with her, she knew, but that didn't make him any less frustrating overall. "Laundry, motherfucker," she said, going extra vulgar just to startle him and prove he wasn't getting the better of her. "It does laundry."

"Your century really does have a machine to replace every servant, don't you?"

"Mostly, yeah."

Henry picked up his bundle of clothes from near the door. Daphne pulled open the closet door that led to their washer and dryer, and watched him eye it warily. It was interesting, which technology interested and delighted him (plumbing, the toaster, everything to do with the kitchen) and which he found suspicious (cars mostly, but apparently also washers and dryers).

"If you're going to be here for a while, it's time you learned how to wash your clothes more often. And the ones Vibol loaned you, too."

"You realize that's entirely unnecessary?"

"I'm not going to be your servant, so yes, you have to learn."

"I meant, laundering your clothes that often feels excessive."

Daphne decided she didn't want to know how often he was used to his clothes being "laundered." He seemed to have adapted to daily showers very easily, and he hadn't been particularly filthy the day he arrived, so maybe his time period wasn't as gross as she thought, but she still didn't really want to think too hard about what unwashed clothes smelled like in the era of horse shit everywhere.

She picked up a basket of underwear and socks that she'd been meaning to wash for several days, and Henry blushed, averting his eyes.

"We'll be washing our things together?"

"I can't imagine your servants washed everyone's clothes separately."

"Likely not, but there's a difference when it's your mother and sisters and when it's you."

"A single woman, you mean?"

"A single woman whom I barely know and whom I find—"

"You probably don't want to finish that sentence," she said, and his mouth snapped shut, but there was an odd look on his face, like he was about to start blushing again.

"Put them in here," she told him, and opened the door to the washing machine. He did as instructed, and she tossed her things in and pulled down the jug of detergent. "Pour about this much into the cap," she said, holding her thumb and forefinger apart.

"What is this?" he asked instead.

"Soap."

"Don't be ridiculous. Soap isn't liquid."

"You know we're able to access entire libraries from our phones, but liquid soap is unbelievable?"

"I've simply never heard of it, that's all."

"You'd never heard of a fucking car, either. Pour the soap, Henry."

He threw her a look but did as she told him, and watched closely as she set the cycle. "I wonder what's happened to the washerwomen," he said. "If these contraptions have put them out of business."

"Um, no idea?" she said. "There's still like, dry cleaners, but that switch would have happened a long time ago. Why do you care?"

He shrugged. "Simple curiosity, I guess. Your world is really—a whole different world for me."

Daphne had another stab of guilt about how cranky she was being with him. "It's not improper here to wash your clothes together. And really, fathers and brothers have like, no say over our lives. Or only do in really fucked-up situations. I get that it's normal for you and your family seems fine with it, but it's not how it is here." Part of her wanted to add *keep that in mind if you ever get back home*, but she didn't want to bring up the fact that, so far, they hadn't even figured out how he'd gotten to the twenty-first century, much less how to get him home.

"My apologies. I meant no offense."

"None taken," Daphne replied. Her shift started in just over an hour, and she was glad she would have a reason to escape from this confusing, confounding man, at least for a little bit.

◆ ◆ ◆

Daphne hoisted the grocery bag higher on her shoulder and opened the door. Henry was on the couch, as was his usual routine these days when one of them was home. He was dressed casually, and other than the fact that he jumped to his feet the moment she walked in, he looked like any other guy she might see on a dating app—relaxed and comfortable.

"Let me help you with that, Miss Griffin," he said, rushing forward to take the bag she had in her hand.

"It's not that heavy," she protested.

Henry stopped trying to take it from her and crossed his arms. "I'm not doing it because I think you're incapable," he snapped.

Daphne sighed, piling the bags onto the counter. "Then why?"

"Because it's impolite to simply wait around while someone struggles with something."

"I was not struggling."

Henry lifted an eyebrow. "You were grunting."

The bags had been heavy, but she hadn't realized her effort was literally showing. "Maybe I just do that, did you ever think of that?"

"You don't."

"How do you know?"

Henry leveled his eyes at her, and suddenly her lungs felt tight. "I notice things about you, my lady."

"Oh, yeah, well," she said inarticulately. She searched in vain for a topic that might make her feel a little less like squirming in the intensity of his gaze. "Any chance you feel like you know me well enough to stop with the 'Miss Griffin' and 'my lady' shit yet?"

Henry huffed out a noise that might have been a laugh and started unpacking the groceries. "No."

"Then how about Dr. Griffin? As a compromise?"

Henry nodded to himself and considered a carton of eggs. "Dr. Griffin," he repeated, and—oh no, that was a bad idea. His Scottish lilt wrapped a little too nicely around those words, and now she wished she could take it back. *Miss Griffin* was annoying as hell, but *Dr. Griffin*, even though people called her that every day, felt somewhat different coming from Henry.

Fortunately, he was too engrossed in studying the eggs to notice her meltdown. "How did you learn how to cook?"

"I don't really know. I guess I didn't, or at least not really. My mom taught me the basics the summer before I went to college, and then I just sort of muddled along. Why?"

"It's not something I ever gave much thought to. Food generally just appears at mealtimes for me at home, and yes, I know how that sounds," he added before she could. "My mother handled menu planning with the cook and the other servants, but other than having some particular favorite dishes, I never really considered it and the effort it takes."

Daphne wasn't sure how to respond to that, as yes, it did sound incredibly entitled, but at least he seemed to get that. "Would you want to learn?"

"To cook? You just said you don't really know how."

"I mean, I do know some stuff, but it isn't something I really enjoy. Except—hey, have you tried watching TV?"

Henry shot a wary glance at their television. "No, it feels like too much."

"Okay, I have an idea," she said, and walked over, turning it on and clicking through the apps. "This show is on PBS, which is—god, I don't know how to explain it, but it means it will be a little less intense than other shows. Calmer, less interested in selling you stuff. Educational."

"That sounds interesting," he said cautiously.

Daphne picked a show at random and hit "Play." "Here, this will teach you about cooking better than I can. I promise," she said as the host began the cheerful introduction to the topics for the episode.

Henry sat down, his attention already off her and fully on the show, which was what she'd wanted, although that also felt weird.

She couldn't wait for him to get back to his time and stop throwing her so goddamn off balance. Daphne returned to putting the groceries away, and just when she was sure he'd forgotten she was even there, Henry turned her way. "Miss—Dr. Griffin?"

"Yeah?"

"Thank you," he said, so sincerely she wasn't sure how to respond. Instead she just bit her lower lip to keep from smiling and nodded.

Chapter Eleven

"He's from the past—he's not a dog," Ellie said. "We can just explain to him where stuff is."

"He's literally never done anything for himself, ever."

"He's standing right here, you know," Henry interjected mildly.

"Have you ever made a meal for yourself? With your own two hands?" Daphne asked.

"When the cook has her afternoon off, I have assembled a sandwich, yes."

"See?" Ellie said. "He can handle a sandwich. We'll put everything out for him, even. Literally all of us are on call today, so it's not like we have another choice."

"I have even been known to open a cupboard, if the situation calls for it."

"Then what's he going to do all day?"

"Again, he's a human, not a corgi. He won't pee on the carpets if we're gone for twelve hours. We've got books."

"I repeat, I am right here, part of this conversation." Henry crossed his arms, now in a white T-shirt Vibol had given him. Daphne looked away, mostly on account of those goddamn biceps. She'd seen Vibol in that shirt before, but that hadn't made her stomach flip.

Ellie gestured at him. "See? We could even set him up with like, YouTube or something. Let him learn about modern life."

Daphne kept her gaze on her roommate. "You want to leave a white man from the nineteenth century alone with the white-nationalist radicalization machine?"

"Okay yeah, good point," Ellie said, making a face. "We can make a Netflix list for him, let him learn about life through our algorithm, not theirs."

"Can't I just read?" Henry asked. "I don't much fancy working with logarithms."

"That's not what we meant," Daphne said. "And no, we can't explain what we did mean. And you could read, yeah, but if you're going to be here for a while, you might as well immerse yourself in our culture."

Ellie went to their TV to pick what she felt would be the "most helpful" movies for him, while Daphne walked him through where he could find bread, sliced turkey, and cheese for a sandwich.

"Henry, have you ever read Jane Austen?" Ellie called from her perch on the couch.

"My sisters made sure of it," he replied.

"Aren't your sisters younger than you?" Daphne asked.

"They are. Both are blessed with quite forceful personalities," he said. "You'd like them."

A flash of sadness crossed his face and Daphne averted her eyes, feeling like she was suddenly intruding. She wanted to say something, maybe something gentle like *you must miss them*, but then Ellie called him over to explain how remotes worked and the moment passed.

◆ ◆ ◆

Ellie looked positively invigorated when they left the hospital just over twelve hours later, but Daphne felt, as usual, almost dead on her feet. Nothing had gone wrong, other than the usual ER chaos, but she felt drained and like she wanted to cry, while Ellie excitedly listed all her accomplishments. Daphne leaned against the window of the light-rail as they rode home, watching the lights of the city flicker past.

"I'll make the pizza if you want to shower," Ellie offered as they approached their door. "And I'll deal with him, since you look like you need a break."

Daphne did need a break. Possibly a weeklong one where she was unconscious, just to feel like she'd recovered from the exhaustion of doing her dream job. She pushed their door open and stopped, leaving Ellie to smack right into her back, because—had she fallen asleep? Was she so unbelievably tired that she was hallucinating? Had she actually hit her head when she crashed into Henry, and now she was experiencing the delayed results of that TBI?

Because Henry was standing in their kitchen, wearing an *apron*. Daphne hadn't even known they owned an apron, but there he was, wearing one and looking positively delighted.

"What's the 411, ladies?" he asked.

"Um, what?" Daphne said, tossing her keys to the side.

"What's happening?"

"Henry, are you—okay?" Ellie asked.

"Totally awesome," he replied. "I made you dinner."

"You made dinner?" Daphne asked. "Do you know how?"

"As if," he said, and something clicked into place.

"Did Ellie have you watch *Clueless*?"

"She did. And I figured out how to make those pizzas you love."

"You did? How?" Daphne looked at the oven, but there wasn't any smoke coming out of it, at least.

Henry sent her an annoyed look that was rapidly becoming familiar. "The instructions are on the packaging. Quite ingenious, that wrapping is. What sort of paper is it made from that it's so transparent?"

"It's plastic."

"What Regina is made of?"

Daphne stared at him blankly, while Ellie cracked up. "You made it all the way up to *Mean Girls*? Dang, you watched a *lot*."

"I confess I have some questions about, ah, let's say, contemporary femininity. But I understand that Cher and Tai's movie is considered old now?"

"Yeah, it's more of a classic. *Mean Girls*, too," Daphne said. "What else did you have him watch, El?"

"Mostly stuff he might recognize the plot in. So *Clueless, Ten Things I Hate About You*—"

"Absolutely delightful interpretation of Shakespeare, that one," Henry interrupted. "My friend George loves Shakespeare, which I never really understood until seeing Patrick and Kat argue on-screen. But *Clueless* was brilliant. Peerless. My sister Anne would adore it, along with the lack of petticoats. Maggie too, for that matter."

"What was *Mean Girls* for, then? That's not an adaptation of a novel."

"That was for feminism, baby," Ellie said.

Henry nodded. "I did not realize *whore* was considered offensive here. I shall try to remember that."

"To be fair, I'd be surprised if it wasn't at least a little pejorative in your time," Daphne said, but she lost her battle with a smile as he grinned back at her.

"As if," he repeated.

"We're going to have to work on your use of that. How long has the pizza been in?" Ellie asked.

Henry looked at the clock above the stove. "Ten minutes."

The thought of getting to eat as soon as she got home from work, without having to do anything or even order it, made her go all melty inside, even if it was just yet another frozen pizza. "I'll make a salad," she offered, suddenly feeling more energized than she had all day.

◆ ◆ ◆

Having a third roommate from the nineteenth century was weird, to say the least. For one thing, he didn't pay rent—although to be fair, he was sleeping in Helen's apartment—and while he did try to make them food when they were at work, his efforts were pretty hit or miss.

Nearly a week after his arrival, Daphne found herself with a day off while Ellie had to work a whole shift, plus stay on-call for the next twelve hours. Brittany was out training for her marathon, Michelle had something to do at her uncle's place, and Vibol was—somewhere. Daphne wasn't sure where, but he wasn't home. Usually, there was at least one more person around to hang out with Henry, which helped keep him from under Daphne's skin. But that day, after she grabbed her finally fixed bike from the shop, she was out of excuses and reasons to avoid him.

They were in the Central Library, tucked into a table set back near the Occult Nonfiction section, desperately trying to find *something* that might give them a clue how to get him home.

Which meant Daphne was spending her day off reading a bunch of vaguely scientific-sounding nonsense about the "metaphysical energy of specific rock formations."

Granted, the man sitting across from her *had* time-traveled from almost 150 years ago, so perhaps she should be less skeptical of the supernatural. But they had also been reading for two straight hours without any real luck, aside from a footnote Henry found that claimed specific moon phases could "influence the flow of time, as with the tides."

The man himself sighed and slammed the book he was reading (*Astrology and You: The Basics*) shut. "This is horseshit," he snapped.

Daphne blinked. She hadn't ever seen him quite this angry before—he'd been haughty, and irritating, and irritated, but never furious. Frustrated, perhaps, but never angry. "I can't—fuck this, I need to get out of here," he growled, and shoved back from the desk. He stalked to the front, and Daphne hurried to follow him. Henry had stopped being quite so freaked out by cars, but she still didn't think he could handle a city street unaccompanied.

"Henry," she hissed, sending an apologetic wave to the librarian at the reference desk as she followed him outside. "Where are you going?"

"I don't *fucking* know," he spat, and she reeled back.

"Okay, good luck then. Hope you know how to get home," she said coolly.

"Wait, Miss—Dr. Griffin," he said, and grabbed her wrist. Not hard, but enough to stop her from returning to the library. "Please. Forgive me."

Daphne looked from his hand on her arm to his face, taking in the sudden desperation. As always, she was a sucker for a wounded bird. "What happened?"

He took a deep breath. "I was reading about moon phases and constellations, and I just—I have a family. A family who *needs* me, no matter what you might think of my treatment of them. I have friends, and a business, and a life, and I don't—I might not—"

"You're worried you're stuck here forever."

"Yes," he said, and it was as if the word had been wrenched from him against his will.

Her heart softened a little more. "Let's take a break, then. I'll go put our books back, and then we can take a walk."

He nodded, and when she came back outside, she found him leaning up against the wall of the library, face to the sun, eyes shut.

"Henry? Are you okay?"

He chuckled, eyes still closed. "No, I'm not all right. But thank you for asking nevertheless."

He fell into step beside her as she started walking, not asking where they were going. Daphne started steering them toward the river, which was just a few blocks ahead. She called on her Doctorsona, even though she had precious little time to spend at patients' bedsides. "Can you tell me about your family? Would that help?" she asked.

"Perhaps."

Perhaps was not a *no*, so she kept going. "What are they like?"

He kept his eyes on the sidewalk. "It's just my mother and my sisters," he said. "Like I told you the first day, my father passed when I was young. Influenza. Is that—do you have that, still? Or is it like smallpox?"

"We still have it, but we have inoculations against it. They're not perfect, but that and some medicines make it much, much easier to beat."

A slight pause. "You are fortunate, then."

"We are," she agreed.

"My father owned an import firm, and after he passed, my uncle ran it. It was quite successful under my father's leadership, and my uncle was a capable enough caretaker, so we were fortunate. I was born in a small house just outside Edinburgh, but just before Father died and shortly after Anne was born, we moved into a much grander home in the city itself. I took over MacDonald's Imports once I was old enough, and at the very least I haven't squandered Father's hard work."

"Do you like it?"

"The company is my responsibility," he said, both answering and not answering the question at the same time.

"What about your mom? And sisters?"

Henry sent her a weak smile that hurt to look at. "Maggie is two years younger than me, and Anne was born when I was ten."

"Are they married?"

"No."

"I swear I'm not making fun—I just don't know the answer—but didn't people back then get married at like, sixteen? Or at least girls?"

"As if," he said, with another faint smile. "Did I use it correctly?"

"Mostly," she confirmed.

"Most ladies of their age are married, yes, although generally not by sixteen. I understand you and your friends are not unusual in your time in being unmarried at your age, but women in my time do marry younger. Some nobility might have their daughters marry that young, but we're not aristocrats."

"You're not wealthy? I thought you just said you were."

"We are, or were, I guess. But I mean it in the social-standing sense. My father was a commoner; therefore we are commoners, unless Anne were to marry someone of noble rank."

"Why not Maggie? Or you?"

"I am not someone the aristocracy deems suitable," he said glumly. There was a story there, she could tell, but whatever it was, he didn't want to share it.

"And Maggie? Is she also 'unsuitable'?"

"Maggie has informed me she will not marry until women are allowed to own property in their own right, separate from their husbands." He stole a look at her. "I know you believe me to be an unbearable boor, but I would never force my sisters to do something they didn't want to do."

"I don't find you unbearable," Daphne argued.

"But you do find me to be a boor?"

"Even you have to admit, you have your moments."

Henry flashed her a smile that didn't quite reach his eyes.

"It sounds like Maggie's a bit of a handful?"

"They're both absolute hellions," he said, shaking his head fondly. "Maggie has quite the head for numbers, and I think she would like it here. More possibilities for her, anyway. Anne spends all her time reading, but mostly loves playing pranks on me."

"Not on Maggie?"

"No, only me," he said, and returned her soft smile. They stopped halfway across the bridge overlooking the Mississippi, and he leaned back against the railing. "Maggie would have her head if she even thought about it. Sometimes Anne teases George too, since he's been like a brother to her for as long as we can remember."

"It sounds like you miss them," she said gently.

"Your patients must be very lucky, to have a doctor who cares this much," he said, rather than answering her question.

"I don't really have the time to talk to most of them," she admitted. She rested her forearms on the railing, looking out toward the river while he faced the road behind them.

"Sounds as though you wish it were otherwise."

"American health care is all fucked up, yeah."

"So much I've gathered. But I meant that it sounds as though you're unhappy."

"I'm not," she said, probably a little too quickly. "It's what I've always wanted."

Henry looked at her, his gaze unsettling. It was like he could see inside her, see things even she didn't want to look at. And even worse, he wasn't looking away, disgusted, or appalled. He simply looked at her, like who she was, deep down, was interesting.

She couldn't take it anymore. "We should get back."

Henry looked as though he were about to say something, but then he closed his mouth and shook his head. "Daphne?" he said, and as he'd never used her given name, her heart skipped a beat at the irregularity of it all. "Are we friends now?"

"Do you want to be?"

His eyes seemed to glow in the midafternoon light. "I think I'd like that, Daphne. I'd like that very much."

And Daphne was left to ponder if it was the strangeness of having him use her given name that made her heart beat like that, or something else entirely.

Chapter Twelve

"Okay, now that the water's boiling, you just pour the pasta in, but be ready to stir or it'll boil over."

"That's it?"

"That's it," Daphne confirmed.

Henry did as instructed, although his face remained dubious.

It was another day where Ellie had to work but Daphne was off, which meant spending time with Henry.

Ever since that day at the library, it felt like something critical between them had shifted, and now rather than dreading it, she was looking forward to it. Being around Henry wasn't always easy, but she felt like she understood why he could be so difficult. Picking apart what was because he was living in an entirely unfamiliar century and what was just him being an arrogant dick was tricky, but Daphne was getting better at it.

Questioning her every suggestion when she instructed him on how to make spaghetti? That was due to being baffled by everything, including dried pasta and electric stoves. Haughtily informing her that his cook made far superior dishes back in 1885? That was, unfortunately, all Henry. Even stranger was that he was growing on her, arrogance and everything. He was, she had to admit, charmingly interested in new experiences, like the drag brunch Brittany and Ellie had taken him to the previous weekend while Daphne was stuck at the hospital.

"Tell me, Daphne," he said, and there was still the slightest hesitation before he said her first name, like he had to remind himself of what to say. "What's your favorite food?"

"Milkshakes," she said without thinking. They hadn't introduced him to fast food yet, although he had seen mentions of it in his diligent movie watching.

"Is that something I—we could make?"

"Not the ones I love. We'd have to go out and buy it."

"Would you take me?"

"Like, now?"

He smirked, and she felt a familiar, if faint, flare of irritation. "That would be wasteful, seeing as I'm in the middle of cooking dinner."

"You're cooking?" she teased, earning herself a grin. "I thought *we* were cooking."

"You're merely supervising," he said with a haughty sniff.

"How about dessert, then? We eat the spaghetti, and then go get milkshakes?"

Henry grinned at her again, so warmly and genuinely Daphne had to look away.

◆ ◆ ◆

It wasn't warm enough yet for the local ice cream stores to open—that wouldn't happen for another month or so—but the spring evening was pleasant enough that having milkshakes from a national franchise that nearly shared Henry's last name while sitting outside wasn't terrible.

The patio was small, mostly full of families with little kids and a handful of teenagers celebrating it being Friday. Henry was a little confused by the straw at first, and then irritated by how difficult it was to drink a milkshake through one, but eventually he got the hang of it (or enough ice cream had melted to make it a little more drinkable). "And these are common?" he kept saying. "Truly?"

"Truly," Daphne said with a genuine smile. "You should 'invent' these when you get back to Edinburgh; you'd make a fortune."

"I know I'm penniless here, but I am quite wealthy back then," he said teasingly. "Besides, I have now watched *three* movies about time travel, and if Marty McFly has taught me one thing, it's not to meddle in the past."

"Fair enough," Daphne said, taking her cup and his to go throw them out. An older man wandered out of the bar down the street and caught her eye, giving her an uncomfortably lecherous once-over. Daphne turned away, but rather than keep walking, the guy stopped.

"Aw, come on, smile," he said, and Daphne rolled her eyes. The man snapped, "Hey, I was talking to you."

Daphne didn't flinch, but Henry was at her side so quickly it was as if another portal in the space-time continuum had opened up. "Do not speak to her like that," Henry growled, and the man—a skinny white man in a suit, probably somewhere around fifty and clearly not used to being told what to do—stopped in his tracks. Henry pressed his advantage, stepping out onto the sidewalk. "Do you always speak to ladies like that?"

"Henry, it's not—" Daphne protested, but he kept his eyes on his target.

"I asked you a question," Henry said, his voice dipping dangerously. "Do you speak to ladies like this often?"

"I don't—"

"Then apologize," he snapped. "Now."

"I, um, I'm sorry . . . miss?"

Daphne nodded and Henry stepped back, relinquishing the man from his captive gaze. The man scurried—*scurried*—away, and Daphne took a breath to return her heart rate to normal. Usually she ignored men like that, preferring to just go about her day as if she'd gone temporarily deaf. "Are you okay?" Henry asked, now sounding worried.

"It was nothing," Daphne said, tossing her hair over her shoulder. "Really, happens all the time."

"It shouldn't," he said softly. They started walking slowly back toward their apartment building, the sun rapidly setting and a chill creeping in. "I thought you said—never mind."

"What?"

"Can I ask something without you arguing with me about it?"

"Can't promise that, no, but you should ask anyway," Daphne said wryly, the brief adrenaline rush of earlier already draining from her system.

Henry huffed out a laugh. "You said that women are more respected now, but that didn't seem like it."

"That's not a question," she said, and wrapped her arms around herself. She had goose bumps, but whether it was from the loss of adrenaline or the cool spring evening, she couldn't say.

"A gentleman would never dream of doing that in 1885," he said. Henry shrugged off his sweatshirt and draped it over her shoulders, ignoring her feeble protests.

Daphne snorted. She fought the urge to snuggle into his sweatshirt, which was delightfully warm. *He's just trying to be polite,* she reminded herself. "That's what you think, but come on, do you really believe that?"

"I would never dream of speaking to a woman like that."

"Of course you wouldn't, because you're a decent person. You were decent in 1885, and you're decent now. But think of the absolute shittiest man you can imagine, and ask yourself if he truly respects women. And not just ladies of your status or whatever, but poor women, too."

Henry fell silent. "You're probably right."

"Who are you thinking of?"

"Jeremy Nash. I went to school with him, and he had a nasty habit of bothering the servants."

"See? You even knew about him, but I'm betting he never did anything out of line with women of your status, right?"

"You're right," he said, brow furrowed. "Did I overstep back there? Should I have let you—what's that phrase you use—handle it?"

"Usually I just ignore them, because guys like that are cowards, you know? They want the reaction, and they get mad if there isn't one. And most of the time it's not worth it. But it was nice, having you stand up for me."

Henry smiled back at her and grabbed the door handle to their building, raising his eyebrows when she went to protest. "Let me do this, Daphne," he said softly, and she bit her lip, wondering just how deep she was getting.

Chapter Thirteen

Daphne stifled a jaw-cracking yawn and nodded to Michelle, who was headed to her day shift at the OB clinic. Daphne had spent the night at the hospital—a blessedly uneventful shift, for once, just the usual moderate chaos—and was really looking forward to collapsing into her bed until midafternoon. She was halfway through daydreaming about her pillow—so soft, so perfect—when she opened the door and jumped about half a mile.

Henry stood in the middle of their living room, a paperback clutched in his left hand, looking expectantly at her. It wasn't so much his presence, since she knew he had a key now, and more that she wasn't expecting to see him so goddamn *early*.

"I'm sorry, I didn't mean to frighten you," Henry said with an odd, overly excited-looking smile. "Ellie's still asleep, but I simply had to talk to someone."

Daphne yawned again. "About what?"

"This. I found it in Helen's apartment," he said, and held up the paperback. It was older and clearly well loved, if the cracks on the spine were anything to judge by.

Daphne squinted. "I hate to break it to you, but *Jurassic Park* will not help us with time travel."

"It's not that. It's—is this real?"

Daphne had had to function at an extremely high level for twelve brutal hours, and her brain just straight up didn't work anymore. "I have no idea what you mean, I'm sorry."

"The science in it. Is this real?"

"Like, DNA? Yeah, that's real," she said, toeing off her shoes. If Henry weren't around she'd probably just strip out of her scrubs and throw them straight into the wash, but he'd nearly had a heart attack from the idea of her washing her underwear with his clothes. Stripping down to her underthings would probably kill him on the spot.

"No, the science. All of it."

Daphne stopped in her tracks, doing her best to keep a straight face. "You mean, do we have dinosaurs?"

"Yes," he said, and then took another look at her. "But given the grin you're failing to hide, I'm assuming I'm wrong."

She gave up. "You are, I'm sorry." She tilted her head to the side as a rueful smile spread across his face. "Did you think you were going to get to see dinosaurs?"

"Well, excuse me for thinking I'd get to see one of God's most majestic creatures. You do have contraptions that take people to the stars, you know. To me, that's equally difficult to comprehend," he protested, but he was starting to chuckle while Daphne burst into giggles. She was doing her best to stay quiet—Ellie slept like the dead, but she didn't want to risk waking her anyway—but the giggles were slowly winding up and out of control.

"I'm sorry, but how—how far did you get in that book?"

"The first few chapters."

Daphne's giggles were full-on laughter now, and Henry was grinning broadly. "You'll want to read—a little further," she said between cackles.

Ellie came out of her room in her bathrobe, yawning. "The hell is so funny this early?" she asked with good humor.

Henry was laughing too, now, and held up the book as if that were an explanation.

"He—he thought—he thought it was—" Daphne stammered, gasping for air.

Ellie looked at the book and wrinkled her nose. "Aww, did Henry think we had dinosaurs in the twenty-first century?"

"Again—you've been to the moon," he protested, still laughing.

"Fair enough," she said, shoving her hair back from her face with her hand. "Come on, Henry, I'll show you how to make scrambled eggs."

Chapter Fourteen

Daphne and Brittany were sitting on the couch, listlessly scrolling through half a dozen streaming services, unable to decide what to watch, when Vibol walked in like a sitcom character from the 1990s, without even bothering to knock.

"Michelle is home from her shift soon," he announced without preamble.

"You should knock—we could have been naked," Daphne called without looking back.

"Good thing you weren't, or Henry might have had an aneurysm."

"It would have been challenging, yes," Henry said, following Vibol in, and that got Daphne craning her neck. Vibol had agreed to take Henry out shopping, and—well, Vibol had good taste, that was clear. Henry looked appealing in new jeans and a button-down shirt, and for a second he looked at her and she looked at him until her ears started to feel like they were burning.

"What about this documentary about—" Brittany leaned forward, squinting through her glasses. "Mormon cheerleaders who started a cult?"

"Oh, I want to watch that, for sure," Ellie said as she came out of her room. "But why are the guys here?"

"Michelle's off soon," Vibol repeated.

The rest of the women exchanged a look. "What does that have to do with us?"

"Um, we're all going to be around and off work for at least twenty-four hours? Isn't that like, unprecedented?"

"Probably," Ellie said. She pulled a bag of pretzels from the pantry and passed them wordlessly to Vibol after taking a handful. "What do you have in mind?"

"As tempting as, uh, cult-leader cheerleaders is, I was thinking something more exciting."

"Hard to think of something more exciting than that," Brittany said.

"I was thinking we should go out," Vibol said. "Maybe Benny's?"

Brittany screwed up her face. "Eww, Benny's?"

"Did you have a better suggestion?"

"Speakeasy?" Ellie offered.

"Michelle hates Speakeasy," Vibol pointed out.

"Do we know if she wants to come?" Daphne asked. "Isn't she still at the hospital?"

Vibol sniffed. "I know what Michelle likes, and she *hates* Speakeasy."

The women exchanged another look, and this time, Henry joined in. "Well, where does she want to go?" Daphne asked.

"She likes Pour and Blanche's."

"Blanche's has a good DJ on Saturdays," Ellie said, taking the pretzels back from Vibol.

"DJ?" Henry asked.

"Person who . . . plays music?" Daphne said in an attempt to translate.

"The one who picks what you hear, yeah," Ellie said.

"Like the conductor?"

"Kind of?" Daphne said. "The music isn't live, though."

Brittany groaned. "I'll have to shower if we go out, and I was just going to spend the day in my sweats. And I'll have to put in my contacts."

Vibol made a pleading face, and Brittany sighed. "Okay, fine, *but* you have to tell Michelle how you feel."

That made him reel back. "What? I don't—we're just friends, same as you guys."

"Um, you don't pick where we go based on what I like," Brittany argued. "Or else I'd be watching shitty TV in peace, like the good Lord intended."

"No one's forcing you to come," he said around a pretzel.

"Oooh, good swerve," Ellie said.

Vibol chucked a mini pretzel at her head, but Ellie just caught it and ate it. "I have *no idea* what you guys are talking about," he insisted. "Help a bro out, Henry."

"You do appear to have romantic feelings for Miss—Dr. Allen," Henry said. "Your friends are portraying the situation accurately."

"And after I taught you how to roll your sleeves up to your forearms? This is how you repay me? With betrayal?" Vibol replied dramatically. He looked around and shook his head. "You're a bunch of assholes."

"Yes, but assholes who will be your wing-ladies while you attempt to woo Michelle," Ellie said.

Vibol was a smart man, who knew when he'd been beaten. "Fine. Let's meet in the lobby at nine?"

"I'll call the RideShare," Brittany said sympathetically. "You can sit with Michelle in the back and everything."

◆ ◆ ◆

"Are establishments like this always so loud?" Henry said, bending his head to be down near Daphne's ear. A pop song was blasting and Brittany and Ellie were out on the dance floor, while Vibol and Michelle huddled at the other side of the booth, absorbed in their conversation.

"Honestly, yes," Daphne shouted back over the din.

"And you do this often?"

Daphne shook her head. "Not really. The others do, but I'm just not a lot of fun."

"What makes you say that?" Henry said, brow furrowed.

She shrugged. "Experience. And besides, I never really did any of this in college, which is when most people do it."

"Why not?"

"I was too busy studying."

"But you don't need to study anymore," Henry argued. "Why not go have more fun?"

Across the table, Vibol slid out of the booth and held his hand out to Michelle, towing her over to the dance floor. Her dark-brown skin glowed against her turquoise blouse, or maybe that was because of the way Vibol was looking at her.

"Out of practice, I guess."

"Then practice," Henry said simply.

"I don't want to leave you alone, and someone has to watch our stuff," Daphne replied.

"Then we shall wait until the ladies return, and it will be your turn."

Daphne shifted uncomfortably, Henry's bright-blue eyes burning into her. "What did Vibol get you?" she asked, very unsubtly changing the subject.

"An India pale ale."

"Ewww. Those are gross and way too bitter," Daphne said, wrinkling her nose.

"I find it delicious," he said primly. "Tastes like home."

Daphne had another moment where the enormous weight of Henry's situation slammed into her. Absolutely nothing around him was familiar, even the drinks. It must be so confusing and disorienting, and half the time she treated him like an annoyance. "I'm sorry we can't get you back yet," she said, and the corner of his mouth quirked up sadly.

"You are blameless in that, my lady."

Rather than her usual surge of irritation, her stomach clenched. Out on the dance floor, Vibol was now draping Michelle's arms around his neck, and Ellie and Brittany were heading back toward the booth, sweaty and laughing.

"Everything okay?" Ellie asked, looking shrewdly between them. Daphne nodded and busied herself taking a sip from her martini while Henry studied a couple at a table nearby over his IPA. "Okay then, your turn, Granny."

"Henry has to go, too," Brittany announced. "Really experience twenty-first century life by grinding it out on a dance floor."

"What does that entail, exactly?"

"She means dancing," Daphne said. She took another sip and felt the warmth of the alcohol spread through her, softening her limbs.

"I haven't learned your dances," he protested.

"Nothing to learn, you just sorta—bop."

"Bop."

"Just look out there—no one knows what they're doing," Daphne said.

"That isn't very comforting."

"It wasn't meant to be," Daphne said and stood up. The alcohol was making her feel reckless, or maybe it was just the way Henry eyed her low-cut shirt. She'd borrowed it from Ellie, and it hung down in a vee to just between her breasts, a style far more daring than she usually wore.

Henry swallowed hard and stood. "I hope—I cannot be as intimate as that, my lady," he said, nodding toward a couple who were back-to-front with hands roaming and groping.

"I wouldn't want you to be," she said. She almost held her hand out for him but changed her mind at the last second. "Don't worry, we don't need to touch."

"I trust you," he said solemnly, and there went the pack of butterflies in her stomach. Again.

Daphne bit back her smile and, feeling his eyes heavy on her back, walked out onto the dance floor. Henry followed, looking adorably nervous. Vibol and Michelle glanced over, cheering in welcome, and the song bled from one song to another, this one a bright, poppy hit by a female singer. Daphne was admittedly not the best dancer, but she felt brave as she spun to face Henry.

"Just find the beat," she explained.

"How do I do that?"

"Just, uh, listen for it?" Daphne started moving back and forth—bopping, as she'd said—and Henry watched, copying her. Soon enough, he figured it out and grinned proudly.

"What's the song about?" he asked.

"Being a, um, dancer who takes her clothes off?"

Henry's eyes grew wide, and she couldn't help but laugh at him. "This world will never fail to surprise me," he said, shaking his head, but he was smiling broadly. "It's fun, though. She sounds . . . happy."

Daphne was going to say something else, maybe tease him a little, but her two left feet got the best of her and she tripped, lurching abruptly forward. Henry caught her by the elbows almost automatically, setting her upright and then dropping his hands as if he'd been burned.

And he wasn't the only one—where he'd caught her still tingled, as if he'd singed her through the thin fabric of her shirt. It was the most deliberate contact they'd had since she had patched him up after their accident, and Daphne was abruptly all too aware of how much she wanted him to touch her again.

Henry wiped his palms on his jeans, and okay, sure, message received. Daphne redirected her energy to dancing, hoping he didn't notice her awkwardness.

It wasn't his fault she was being weird. She would just have to remember that.

Chapter Fifteen

Slowly, Daphne adjusted to Henry's constant presence in their lives. He liked a challenge, and she appreciated that about him. And even though he was still frequently bewildered by modern life, he had taken to the broader range of food available very quickly. He loved Thai food, which Daphne had introduced him to on a rainy Thursday afternoon, cackling as he hopped around the kitchen searching for milk to manage the spicy burn. Once he'd gotten over that first shock, he proclaimed he loved it, and kept looking for new things to taste and cook.

There was a lack of pretention about Henry that she wouldn't have noticed at first. He was arrogant as all hell—that much hadn't changed from her first impression—but he embraced new ideas and experiences with a lot more equanimity than she would have ever guessed.

Henry squinted at the recipe he had displayed on Ellie's tablet. "Keep stirring," he instructed. "It doesn't look right to me yet."

"Yes, chef," Daphne teased, standing at her station at the stove. The recipe Henry had found was incredibly complex, as it involved making curry from scratch, but their kitchen did smell amazing.

Henry moved next to her and dunked the noodles into the boiling water. Daphne knocked her shoulder into his, and he grinned to himself, shaking his head. "I still don't understand why you think it's so impossible, given that all the disparate elements of the technology exist," Henry said, picking up the thread of an old, now-familiar argument.

"Henry, we can't make dinosaurs."

"So you say. But you can create human—what did you call them?"

"Embryos."

"You can create human embryos in a lab. Wouldn't a reptile be less complex?"

"It's less that we can't, and more that we shouldn't," Ellie said, emerging from her room. She'd been sleeping for most of the day, having pulled an overnight shift every night for the past week. Daphne herself was gearing up for a stretch of those and dreaded it, and not just because of the difficulty of night shifts.

"I still think maybe if they tried with an herbivore—"

"No one has a secret dinosaur island," Daphne said.

"That you know of," Henry argued. "And turn the heat off—that looks done."

Daphne obligingly turned off the heat for the sauce she'd been stirring and turned to face him. "Again, did you bother to finish the book?"

"I did."

"And you still think we should make a dinosaur island? Maybe we should show you the movies."

"Movie. The original slaps. The rest are terrible cash grabs," Ellie said, but Henry didn't look at her.

He turned away from the noodles to face Daphne. "I simply think it's not possible for you to know, definitively, if there's a dinosaur island somewhere or not."

"Okay, but keeping something like *that* a secret would be really hard. There'd be all the scientists, and research scientists might be a bunch of dorks, but they're a *chatty* bunch of dorks. If one of them knew how to make dinosaurs, you couldn't keep them from telling someone about it—"

"Um, guys?" Ellie interjected.

"Money can buy silence," Henry said.

"Not when it comes to something like this. And it's not just the scientists; there would be like, people who feed the dinosaurs, groundskeepers, janitors—"

"Guys?" Ellie tried again.

Henry's eyes glimmered with a smile that didn't reach his lips. "Lots of money can buy a lot of silence," he insisted.

"Sure, but—"

"What about spy satellites? We have those, you know. Governments would know, and if it was someone from a different country, then there wouldn't be incentive to keep it quiet."

"Food's burning," Ellie said.

"For someone who doesn't have a lot of faith in the government, you seem to when it is convenient," Henry replied, and god, those blue eyes were going to kill her.

Daphne crossed her arms over her chest. "I am just being practical about geopolitics."

"Guys," Ellie said loudly.

Reluctantly, Daphne looked away from him. "What?" she said at the same time as Henry.

"Food's burning," Ellie said with a jerk of her chin.

Just then, Daphne caught the acrid scent of water burning on a stovetop as the pot Henry was minding bubbled over.

"Bloody hell," he muttered, whipping it off the burner and blowing on the bubbles to calm it down.

"Is it okay?" Daphne asked.

"Looks okay. Maybe a little overdone but nothing catastrophic. Would you want some for dinner, Ellie?" Henry asked. "We made a peanut curry."

For some reason, Ellie was grinning mischievously. "Sounds delicious."

"What's your deal?" Daphne asked, grabbing bowls from the upper cabinet. "Why are you smiling like that?"

But Ellie just kept grinning like the cat that got the canary. "If you don't know, I'm sure as hell not telling you."

◆ ◆ ◆

"I found something while I was reading in Helen's apartment," Henry said over breakfast a few days later, between bites of scrambled eggs. "I couldn't make sense of it, so I brought it here, to see what you think."

Daphne took the book from him. *The Time Veil*, it said on the spine, although in some places, the gold was flaking off. The fabric hardcover was worn in spots, and the paper inside was yellowed and brittle. The scent of dust and knowledge trickled from the pages as she flipped to the spot he indicated. Most of Helen's books were thrillers, but this looked—different. Strange. Otherworldly.

Daphne read the paragraphs three times, turning the words over in her head.

> *Some liminal spaces are more liminal than others, the veil thinning as the moon reaches the proper position. In these spaces, as suggested by Hoyme, one might be able to shift between times, as stepping through a waterfall. Before, the future, behind, the past. The water is the present, shimmering and ephemeral.*
>
> *These spaces can be found along ley lines, those ancient and hallowed veins of power. With the right moon position on the line and the traveler's birth, it may be possible to step through the waterfalls of time.*

"It sounds like it's talking about time travel, doesn't it?" Henry asked. "And look, there's a map."

Daphne squinted at the small map showing the western hemisphere, crisscrossed with lines that seemed to coalesce into starbursts in places. Along some of the lines were small dots, with symbols she vaguely recognized as belonging to various astrology signs. She could pick out her own, but that was about it. Next to those signs were circles representing phases of the moon, with an arrow and a set of numbers, ranging from 2 to 498.

Ellie peered over Daphne's shoulder. "If those are star signs or whatever, and the phase of the moon, maybe this is like, a code? For when those spaces are open?"

"That's what it looks like, but I don't know what most of those signs mean," Daphne said.

Ellie sat down and scrutinized it closely. "I think the map is showing what sign the moon is in and what phase, maybe when the portal opens? These numbers could be spacing, like how far apart it opens. It looks about right, given what I can see here, at least."

"What else would you need to know?"

"Probably just double-check everything," Ellie said. "But if I'm reading it right, the little space over Minnesota shows it open when the moon is in Virgo, which would be about when he arrived, and then again . . . about a month from now."

Ellie looked up, an odd expression on her face as she glanced between them. One more month, and then Henry could go back. Daphne swallowed hard, willing herself to be excited—he certainly seemed to be—and then caught his eye. Her heart sank, and she had no idea why.

Or maybe she did, and that was even worse.

Chapter Sixteen

Suddenly, it was like there was a ticking clock over everything they did. Daphne could tell he was relieved, and she was, too. Really. Henry deserved to get back to his own time, to his family.

And it would be nice not to be responsible for him anymore, either. Granted, he was a lot more self-sufficient now, and had even started regularly making them meals when they got back from long shifts. It was mostly simple stuff—eggs, pasta, french toast—but it was nice to come home to. He was working hard to understand modern life, and while he had sadly stopped using *as if* constantly and incorrectly, he was coming along. In fact, if Daphne hadn't known already that he was a time traveler, she never would have guessed.

But even though Daphne felt like she was understanding Henry better these days (likes: Kraft Mac and Cheese, showers, and Austen adaptations; dislikes: violent movies, quinoa, and the buzzer that let them know the dryer was done), she still felt like there were parts of him she didn't fully understand.

"Why aren't you married?" she asked one night, having had about half a glass of wine too much. They were sitting on the small balcony that opened out from her bedroom, a soft spring breeze tickling her flushed cheeks. "You're like, old enough."

"Why aren't you?" Henry replied, and okay, yeah, she liked his voice. It was low and rumbly in a way she felt deep down in her belly.

"It's not that weird for a woman to be unmarried at my age anymore."

"And it's not that 'weird' for me to be unmarried at my age, either."

"No, but it's more likely you would be," she argued. "Right?"

Henry sighed into the glass of white wine he'd been nursing. "Right."

"Okay, so, why not?"

"Why aren't you?"

"I asked you first," she said.

Henry sighed again. "I haven't found someone, I guess."

"You guess?"

Henry looked at her, his eyes narrowed. "You're being unbearably nosy."

"Humor me," she said. "You haven't found someone, you said, but then you qualified it. Why?"

"It wasn't that I've never met anyone, as you'd put it. But marriage wasn't an option."

"Why?"

Henry leaned his head back against the chair. "It's a long story. Can I just leave it at that?"

"Fair enough," Daphne said. "But can I ask you another question?"

"Sure," he agreed.

"What do you miss the most? Aside from your family, of course."

He thought for a long moment. "The quiet. And the stars. Even in the city, the lights weren't as bright as these are, so there were more stars. And no infernal motors."

"Infernal motors?" she asked with a grin. "What are you, eighty?"

"Somewhere around my sesquicentennial, actually."

Daphne snorted, and Henry shot her a smile that did something unexpected to her heart. "It sounds nice," she said honestly.

"It is, in some ways."

"Only some?"

"Only some. I don't know how to explain how strange and wonderful it is to me that you can prevent almost any disease."

"Not any," she protested.

"But most. My father died of influenza, and before we moved to our current house, we lived in a middle-class neighborhood that was not too far from housing for laborers. The things I saw, Daphne, the things I know happen every day—you can't imagine it."

"I probably can," she said softly. "I spend my days surrounded by pain."

"But there's hope here. We have some, but not like this. Back home—most of the people you see, they wouldn't have made it to a doctor, much less have a chance. And the babies . . ." He shook his head. "Children die all the time. My own mother lost a babe before me, and she is considered lucky for only having lost one. Here, it's so rare, and I don't know if you understand how miraculous that is."

Daphne hadn't thought about it like that, or at least not in-depth. She believed in medicine and knew that the twenty-first century was able to save people who would have died even sixty years earlier. But she'd never really thought about the way things had changed since the nineteenth century. She cleared her throat, suddenly tight.

"But you miss it, don't you?"

There was a long, long silence. The air between them thickened, and Daphne found she was holding her breath. "Some of it," he said finally.

Do you still want to go back? The words were on the tip of her tongue, but she couldn't bring herself to ask them. Suddenly, the thought of hearing him say *yes, I can't wait* felt painful. "That must be hard," she said instead, falling back on one of her Doctorsona's favorite phrases. It felt cheap, like a cop-out.

"It is. Not as hard as it was at first, though," he said, with a look that felt meaningful.

But what it meant, exactly, she didn't want to consider.

◆ ◆ ◆

It was the night that Daphne always dreaded—her turn to be the resident on call. All the residents were scared of it, since it meant way more responsibility than any of them felt capable of handling, but most of them came out of that shift exhilarated. Uncle Pete's Tavern was having another special, but this time there weren't quite as many college kids stumbling in for a stomach pump and IV of fluids. It was probably getting close to finals, so Daphne guessed they had a week or two of respite while kids tried to study, before the onslaught of graduation.

At least Hannah was the charge nurse for the shift. She had been working in the ER for years and wasn't fazed by anything. If Daphne was frozen with indecision, she could usually count on Hannah to rescue her with a gentle suggestion. The rest of the residents were always assuring Daphne that her anxiety about on-call shifts was normal, that they all felt the same way, and it must be just impostor syndrome. But as Daphne stood in front of a nurse who needed orders for a patient (thirty-seven-year-old female, high fever and dehydration), she couldn't help but feel like it was different for her.

"Influenza test was negative?" Daphne said, frowning. "And no signs of appendicitis. Um, let's do—a broad-spectrum antibiotic and . . . wait, hang on." They were way behind, as usual, and the current wait in the ER was three hours, minimum. But something was humming quietly in the back of Daphne's brain, and she needed to figure it out.

Daphne knocked on the glass door that separated the room from the rest of the ER. The woman inside looked wan, and her brown skin had a sickly, grey cast. She had the look of someone who had lost a lot of weight fairly quickly, and immediately, Daphne's antennae went up.

She pumped the hand sanitizer on and sat down on the stool. "Hi there, I'm Dr. Griffin. Can I ask you a few questions?"

Her patient, Melissa, nodded weakly, and Daphne began the exam. With every answer Melissa gave, Daphne's heart sank further. *No appetite, bloating, family history of cancer.* Everything pointed to ovarian cancer, but she didn't want to scare her before she was sure. She kept a professional mask on and grimly ordered the proper tests, but with how long she had left on her shift—four hours—and how long it would take for Melissa to get up to CT and have a radiologist read the scans, there was almost no chance Daphne would be there to break the news to her patient.

And that, more than anything, was what made her duck into the supply closet for a quick cry. Daphne wanted to be there *with* patients, not just breeze in and out. And she wasn't naive—she understood that this was, for better or worse (and usually worse), the state of health care in the US.

But right then, in that moment, she hated it.

◆ ◆ ◆

There weren't any cases that hard for the rest of her shift, although that didn't mean it was easy. The patient she'd been thinking about on her awful date with Anders was back, still with the persistent cough. She was an elderly woman, and Daphne couldn't help but smile a little at her name when she saw she was her next patient. The ER had a lot of frequent fliers, some because of conditions that were hard to manage, and some because they had nowhere else to go for help. Mrs. Green was a little bit of both—chronic health problems and crappy insurance that meant she couldn't see a specialist. "In a few years I'll get Medicare and it will be easier," she had told Daphne many times.

"Hey there," Daphne said as she walked in. "What brings you in today, Mrs. Green?"

She coughed again. "Same as always, dear. How was that date of yours?"

For one confusing second, she wondered how Mrs. Green knew about Henry, and then for one more confusing second, she wondered what they had done that could be considered a date. Then she remembered—Anders.

"Not great," she said ruefully. "He was more interested in himself than me."

"That's too bad. But I'm sure there's someone else out there," Mrs. Green said between coughs. Unbidden, Daphne's mind went to Henry. "Oh, so there *is* someone," Mrs. Green continued. "I saw that little smile."

Daphne shook her head. "It's complicated."

"How complicated?"

"He's not from here," Daphne said, pulling out her stethoscope and listening to her lungs. "Okay, another breath," she coached, and listened intently.

"So? They've had airplanes for a long time, dear."

Daphne's lips tugged up slightly. "Like I said, it's complicated," she said, and then realized exactly what she was implying.

That maybe, if things were different, she could find herself falling for Henry.

Chapter Seventeen

"I've got it," Ellie announced, coming out of her bedroom. She looked like she'd just won a battle with a vicious foe, her hair all unkempt and her eyes slightly wild. "I know how to get Henry back."

Daphne's stomach jolted unpleasantly. It was what they had all been working toward for the past few weeks, but now she felt vaguely ill, like it was something she was dreading, not anticipating. Sure, she liked him a lot more now, but she still wanted him to get back to his family.

Henry, on the other hand, seemed ecstatic. "Truly?"

"Truly," Ellie said, breathing hard. "I had to do like, *so much math*, but I've got it." She thrust a stack of papers at them, all covered in signs and a series of long equations. "It is ley lines, but whether or not the portal works is also dependent on the person. Henry is a Capricorn sun with a Virgo moon, which, whoa dude, no wonder you're uptight as hell."

"Is that relevant, El?" Daphne asked.

"It is, in that it's like, the worst chart I've ever seen. His to-do lists have to-do lists."

"I don't have any lists?" Henry replied.

"Okay, yeah, that's not important, really—I just needed to explain myself. But if the moon is in Virgo, like it was the day he arrived, there are spots on the ley lines that allow the veil between time and space to rip slightly, but only for someone who has the right star chart. I did Henry's," she said, pointing to one piece of paper, "and then I compared it to that map in the book he found at Helen's. There's a portal between here and Edinburgh that's the right spacing apart for someone with his chart, so I just had to put everything into this equation." Ellie pointed at another piece of paper, this one covered in incomprehensible symbols arranged into a long equation.

"What does it say?" Henry asked, squinting.

"First of all, it says I'm incredibly smart and was able to figure out really complicated math involving astrology, so there's that. But what it says is the portal opens again in ten days, just a little farther down the ley line."

"How far?"

"That will take some more math to figure out exactly, but not that far—it'll be close. But it does look like it will be really quick. What I could get from that book is that the portals are unstable and short."

"*Unstable* sounds bad," Daphne said.

"Not unstable as in dangerous. Just like, it'll show up and then go away right away, so we have to be super precise. But we're really lucky; there's two cracks at this. One opens in ten days, like I thought, and then the next one opens on the solstice, so just a few more months away."

"Both back to Edinburgh?" Henry asked hopefully.

"Edinburgh in 1885 to be precise," Ellie said with a broad smile. "There's one more that I could find, but it doesn't open for seven years."

"But I could be home in ten days?"

"You could. Or in three months, if—"

"Of course I'll go at the earliest opportunity," Henry said. "Do I need to do anything to prepare?"

Daphne's stomach twisted. "What if it's unsafe?" she pointed out, quite rationally in her opinion. "Or wrong?"

Ellie looked at her shrewdly. "Daph, when the hell have I *ever* been wrong?"

"That time you thought you'd look good as a brunette."

"I mean, wrong about something that involves *math* and *being smart*."

"Fair enough," Daphne conceded, but Henry was looking at her with a hard-to-read expression. "What?" she asked him.

"Do you really think she's wrong?"

"No, I'm just trying to be sure—"

"Because you've been very clear since I arrived that I need to get back to my time, and now that there's a chance I can go back soon, you want, what? To be cautious?"

"That's not—"

"I'm going back," he said flatly.

"I didn't—"

"And I don't need your permission," he added, steamrolling right along.

Daphne looked to Ellie for help, but instead of Ellie being appalled at Henry's behavior, she just looked amused. "El, what do you think?"

"Honestly, I think if Henry's got a chance to go back, he should take it."

"But?" Daphne prompted, because she could tell by the way Ellie was looking between them, she wasn't done.

"But if neither of you guys can figure out why you're suddenly so pissed at each other, that's not my problem," Ellie said, and walked back into her room, leaving Daphne and Henry sitting with a stack of undecipherable math equations and more questions than Daphne had ever had in her life.

◆ ◆ ◆

With each day that passed, it was getting harder and harder for Daphne to ignore the truth.

She had feelings for Henry. Real ones, not just the passing "oh, that'd be nice" way she felt about dating in general. She wanted to talk to him when she got back from a shift, craved hearing about his day, wanted to hear him excitedly explain how he'd learned to use the internet to find a new recipe. It was mundane, simple things, like the way he'd rub the back of his neck when he was thinking, or drum his fingers on the counter while flipping through a stack of cookbooks Ellie had rounded up from her aunts. Henry was getting to be a fairly good cook, and kept throwing himself deeper and deeper into it, wanting to try newer things, harder things.

"Do people dance anymore?" Henry asked, but Daphne was only half listening. She was working on a crossword and was stuck on eleven down (*An escape, sort of*) while Henry read some mystery novel he had swiped from Helen's.

"Hmm?"

"Dancing. Do people dance?"

"I mean, yeah, you've seen our movies, and we took you out one night. We dance."

"Not like that. Proper dancing. Real dancing."

Daphne put down the crossword puzzle book that Ellie had gotten her for Christmas, using her pen as a bookmark. "And what, pray tell, is *real* dancing?"

"Waltzing. Doesn't anyone do that anymore?"

"I mean, I know people do. But a lot of us don't know how to do much more than swaying."

"They don't teach it in school?"

Daphne wrinkled her nose. "I had to learn square dancing in school, if that counts?"

Henry's brow furrowed, and a curl fell across his forehead. "Square dancing? Do you—make squares?"

"It's hard to explain," Daphne said. "But to your question, no, we don't really learn dancing in school. I'm sure there are places to learn, but you'd have to seek them out."

"I see," he said, returning briefly to his book. "Actually, no, I don't."

"Look, education here is really underfunded and—"

"It's not that. It's more that dancing is an art, and it's sad that more people don't care."

"It's less that we don't care, and more—I dunno, we don't really have time."

"Pardon my observation, my lady, but it seems you here in the future have nothing but time."

"Um, we're super busy?"

"In some ways. But with all this technology, you really do have more time—you just spend it differently."

"And what, you think we should use it learning to dance instead?"

"I think you're unhappy. And would be happier doing other things."

Daphne chewed on her lower lip, because Henry was looking at her the way he did sometimes, like he was seeing right into her heart and recognizing something she didn't want to look at. "*You're unhappy*, as in, you think *I'm* unhappy? Or just twenty-first-century people in general?"

Those impossibly blue eyes bored into her. "That depends, Daphne. Are you happy?"

God, sometimes she wished she hadn't made him switch to calling her that. *Miss Griffin* was irritating, but it had a distance that didn't make her stomach flip over the way *Daphne* did in his lilting Scottish accent. She swallowed hard and reached for the Doctorsona mask she used at the hospital, the one that kept her feelings from showing. "Are you offering to teach me how to dance?" she said instead of answering.

As usual, she didn't fool him, but he accepted her dodge with grace. "Do you have anything that's a waltz?" he asked, standing up.

Ellie had a stack of vinyl records that she had gotten from an uncle, and a refurbished record player sitting in the corner. Henry had gotten into the habit of using it from time to time, since it was technology that was vaguely familiar to him in a way computers simply weren't.

It had been a long time since Daphne had taken her one music appreciation course to fulfill her arts requirement in college, but she flipped through a mental list of the records they owned and tossed out a suggestion while he pushed the coffee table off to the side. There wasn't a ton of space in their living room, but Henry didn't seem deterred. He slipped her suggested record out of the sleeve and placed the needle on the correct track.

"C'mere," he said, and *shit*, she wished Ellie were home. Her stomach wouldn't stay put, tumbling over and over, and it was so much easier when she was around to act as a buffer.

Daphne took his hand and let him pull her off the couch. The touch of his palm to hers sent a frisson down her spine and suddenly her lungs felt too small, like there wasn't enough oxygen in the universe for her to breathe properly.

"One hand here," he said, placing her hand on his shoulder. "Like this." He took her other hand and there went the tingles again, setting off another round of stomach gymnastics. His hand went to her waist, and Daphne had never quite felt like this, like there was an intimacy between them she'd never experienced. It was silly, considering she was hardly a virgin, but it felt new and unexpected.

Quietly, Henry began counting through the music, explaining the steps and then leading her through them. She wasn't the best dancer, but she caught on quickly enough. The song ended and Henry went and found another one she suggested, and together they waltzed around her living room to a slow ballad she'd once listened to over and over again on her bedroom floor as a middle schooler, pretending she'd felt real heartache and feeling unimaginably grown up.

The seconds blurred together and the rest of the room faded away, until it was just Henry and the way his hand flexed on her waist, the way his eyes kept dipping toward her lips. The way they kept getting closer and closer, despite his initial explanation of the importance of a separation between them.

"This is nice," she said, sounding dazed. She felt dizzy, even though they hadn't really been spinning much. But the world felt strange and unreal, like lights had been extinguished all around them.

"Daphne, I—" Henry looked dazed too, his eyes saying words she couldn't interpret.

They had stopped. Daphne didn't know when that had happened, but now they were standing in each other's arms, frozen in place while Norah Jones sang mournfully in the background. He let go of her waist and cupped her cheek in his hand, cradling her face gently. "This is—I can't—" he stammered.

A key slid into the doorknob, bumpy and metallic, and the handle twisted. Daphne and Henry jumped apart just as Ellie walked in, launching into a story about her shift without preamble. "And then the nurse said—wait, what's up? Were you guys dancing?" she said, interrupting herself.

Henry recovered first. "Daphne didn't know how. I offered to teach her. How was your day? You were saying someone had something stuck? Somewhere?" he said solicitously, but Ellie was looking between them with narrowed eyes.

"Everything okay? You guys seem . . . weird."

"Everything's fine. Keep going," Daphne said.

"Okay, well, Henry, like I said at the start, I'm sorry that this will probably be shocking for you to hear, but a guy came in, claiming he 'fell' on a carrot, and—"

Ellie continued her story, and yes, Henry blushed as she talked, but Daphne had the distinct impression that blush had been building before Ellie walked in.

Even worse, she felt her own ears burning, and it had nothing to do with a carrot up someone's butt.

Chapter Eighteen

"Dr. Griffin?" Hannah prompted. "What do you want us to do?"

Adrenaline flooded Daphne's veins as she tried to breathe through the panic, the beeping of the machines reminding her of the incredibly high stakes. She wished there were someone else around—Ellie, the chief resident, literally anyone else—but it was just her.

Her, the nurses, and a coding patient. She made her choice and sprang into action, forcing aside the second-guessing clawing at her gut. The room turned into a hurricane of activity, with Daphne standing in the center of it. It was, theoretically, the sort of moment she was supposed to want. This is what people in Emergency Medicine liked to do, what they went into it for. It was what *she* went into it for.

But an hour later, with the patient sent up to surgery but still unlikely to make it much longer, Daphne sank to the floor. She didn't even have the energy to go hide in the closet like she usually did. She just slid down the wall and hid her face in her hands, trying to keep from sobbing. Telling the patient's family that they were "doing what they could" in the most comforting way possible had felt like swallowing knives, because she could tell the wife knew. She knew her wife wasn't going to make it, but she was going to cling to the gossamer thread of hope Daphne was dangling, because in the end it was all they had.

That woman's face, drawn and grey, kept hovering behind Daphne's eyes. No amount of digging the heels of her palms into her eye sockets could get rid of it. It was there, along with the pained cries she knew would follow when the surgeons came down to give her the news Daphne knew was coming. A car crash, with those injuries—you didn't come back from that. They could keep her going, maybe for an hour, maybe long enough that the wife could get upstairs to say goodbye, but the finality of all of it threatened to swamp Daphne.

It wasn't that she wasn't prepared for this. It was something everyone going into medicine knew, because the entire reason people became doctors was to fight against the inevitability of death. Daphne couldn't have gotten through med school without knowing that part of her job would be delivering hard news, sometimes devastating news, and she'd lost patients before. But for some reason this patient, on this day, was just too much.

Daphne gave herself five minutes to drown in self-pity, then dragged herself upright. She had a shift to finish, after all.

◆ ◆ ◆

Daphne made it through the rest of her shift, but how, she couldn't say. She could have sworn she heard the anguished cries when the surgeons told her patient's family she didn't make it, even though that wasn't really possible. The waiting room was upstairs and the emergency room was its usual cacophony of noise, but she knew when it happened all the same.

Henry was sitting on their couch, reading a book, when she came home. "How was work?" he asked conversationally. "Ellie's out for the night. She said not to expect her back until tomorrow."

Daphne nodded, her throat suddenly thick. Henry had turned back to his book, but when she didn't reply, he looked up. "Is everything okay?"

Is. Everything. Okay. Daphne shook her head, the tears burning her eyes. She blinked rapidly. "It's nothing."

"Doesn't look like nothing," Henry said softly. "What happened?"

What happened. Two words, and she shattered. That was when the sobs came. They started in her chest, clawing their way to the surface with serrated, tearing gulps.

She didn't even realize he had stood up, but then suddenly he was holding her, letting her cry against his chest. "It's okay," he murmured into her hair. "It's okay."

Daphne shook her head again, her face rubbing against his shirt. "It's not," she keened. "And it won't be."

He curled his hand protectively around the back of her head and tucked her under his chin. The grief kept swamping her; one wave would recede, and then the next was on top of her before she could catch her breath. And through it all Henry held on to her; somehow understanding that if he let go, she'd drown.

Slowly he coaxed her onto the couch, tucking a blanket around her legs. Daphne kept weeping, but the worst of the storm had passed, replaced by an endless flow of tears. She furiously wiped at her cheeks, while Henry bustled around the kitchen. He joined her on the couch a little while later with a cup of tea that he pressed into her hands over her objections.

"I'll be fine," she said, even though she'd been insisting as much for the past five minutes to no avail.

"I'm sure you will be," Henry said quietly. He nodded toward the cup of tea. "And that will help."

"You're unbelievably English sometimes," she said with a weak smile.

A grin flickered across his face. "I'll have you know I'm Scottish," he protested.

"Like I could forget," she replied. She wiped another tear from her cheek and sniffed.

"Drink your tea," Henry said. "I promise it'll help."

She didn't really feel like drinking or eating anything, but the warmth of the mug was making her hands feel less shaky, so she did as he said. It wasn't anything special, just the tea Ellie had grabbed on their grocery run a few weeks ago, but warmth bloomed inside her as she swallowed. Daphne hadn't even realized she was cold.

"It does," she said over the rim of the mug.

"Imagine that," he said. "Do you want to talk about it?"

Daphne shrugged and stared into the mug. "It was just a bad day. Nothing I can't handle." The lie felt thin and flimsy on her tongue, but now that the worst had passed, she felt ashamed. These sorts of days were something she had trained for, and she knew that even the most hardened emergency doctors had days where it hit them hard. There were steps for her to take, a routine to let the grief flow through her until she felt more grounded. She had helped her friends through these moments before, and knew exactly what she needed to do.

But even when she'd tried to reach for those tools on the way home, she hadn't been able to touch them.

"It must be hard, seeing death so often," Henry said, and his blue eyes were so soft, so understanding, that she had to look away.

"It's not easy," she admitted.

"In my time, there's a lot more death. It's different here, I think. People—see it less."

"It's my job to see it, though. Or fight it, I guess, but sometimes we lose, even with all our skills and technology," Daphne said, swallowing back a sob that threatened to reemerge.

"It doesn't make it easier, though," Henry replied. "Death is death, and seeing it hurts."

The tears pricked her eyes again. "It does, yeah."

Henry gave her another one of his long, searching looks. "I don't think that's what hurts you so much, however."

"Of course it is. Today was—awful."

"I didn't mean it like that," Henry hastened to say. "I meant it's not the only thing upsetting you."

"What else would it be?"

There he went again, searching her face like he wanted her to say something specific. Absurdly, she thought about the fact that he was leaving soon, and her stomach twisted. "You're not happy, Daphne."

"Of course I'm not, I've been sobbing on you for the past hour."

"That's not what I meant. Your job—you're not happy in it."

Daphne snapped her head up. "Of course I am. It's what I've worked for my whole life."

"You're half right," he said, and she felt a surge of her old irritation with him. He was looking at her like he knew something she didn't, and the arrogance she thought he'd left behind was back.

"Oh yeah? Please, enlighten me," she said.

"You worked for this job your whole life, but you're miserable there. And I know, because I was miserable at mine."

Daphne blinked. "You were?"

His smile was sad. "We never really talked about it. But yeah, I never liked it. Or don't, I guess. I still never know what tense to use, but imports was never very interesting. It's a lot of lists, and weighing things, and comparing the weights to the list, and counting. I bloody hated it."

"I guess—I just assumed you guys didn't think about it like that, back then."

"You thought we didn't have hopes and dreams in the past?" he asked, amused.

"I didn't mean it like that. I just meant—it didn't sound like you had much choice. Your dad's firm, and all."

"And I didn't. Doesn't mean I wouldn't have liked to have a say. But that's not really the point—the point is, I know what it's like when your job is slowly draining the life out of you. I know, because I've seen it in the mirror, and I see it on you now."

Suddenly, the tears were back. Daphne tried to rub them away, but they just kept coming, thick and hot down her cheeks. "I can't hate it. I worked too hard to hate it," she said, hiccuping. "It's all I've ever wanted."

"That doesn't mean it's what you want now," he said softly. Henry leaned forward and used his thumb to catch a tear. He traced her cheekbone, cupping her face for a moment before leaning back. "I know from what you all have said that it's expensive to become a doctor, but you can't let that keep you in something you hate. Not if you have another choice."

"I don't hate all of it. I like being a doctor, I really do."

"But not the kind of doctor you are."

The words hung between them. Daphne would've thought someone saying that would send her into a spiral, but instead, she felt calm. Like she could breathe for the first time in years. Like the room had finally stopped spinning. She nodded. "No. Not this kind of medicine."

"So quit."

Daphne stared at him. "You cannot be serious."

"You don't have a family to provide for, and you're bright. I'm sure you could find something else."

"But I don't *want* something else. I want to be a doctor."

"Do you?" he asked mildly.

"I do," she repeated. "I just think I need something quieter. Something where I can talk to patients more, so when things go wrong, I'm not just a stranger giving them the worst news of their life. But it's not that simple."

"Why isn't it? You're still in training, aren't you?"

"Yeah, but the process is really complicated. There's interviews and Match Day and I'd have to give up a year, go back and start over."

"A year, or the rest of your life. Doesn't seem like much of a competition," he said, and even though Daphne didn't think she had any more tears left to shed, she started crying again. She crumpled against him, and once again Henry held her through the storm, his arms safe and comforting even though she'd barely ever touched him before. Dimly she wondered about that, what had changed that his previous reserve had gone by the wayside. But the bigger part of her was just glad to have someone to hold on to as the world completely reoriented around her.

"You can do it, Daph," he said into her hair. "You're stronger than anyone I've ever met."

She shook her head against his shoulder. "If that were true, I wouldn't be thinking about leaving."

There was a long, heavy moment of silence. "Sometimes, walking away is the hardest thing you can do."

Henry shifted, drawing her further across his chest and wrapping his arms more securely around her. The tears had started to ebb, but exhaustion rolled through her. The stress of her shift and the emotional turbulence made her eyelids heavy, and Henry's steady heartbeat and warmth melted her last shreds of awareness.

Chapter Nineteen

Daphne blinked awake, momentarily disoriented. Things came back to her in snatches—falling asleep against Henry, then half waking up in his arms as he carried her to her room. She was alone in bed, still in the clothes she had worn home, her other pillow untouched. The rest of the evening came back to her all at once, and her stomach sank, remembering her grief and their conversation.

But considering a new career track felt far too big to think about without coffee. She padded out of her bedroom and drew up short, because there, on her and Ellie's couch, was Henry.

He was sound asleep, his arm dangling off the side. The blanket was thrown over his legs, and she smiled softly to herself. She tugged the blanket up over his chest and tiptoed into the kitchen.

Daphne watched Henry sleep while the coffee maker burbled, his broad chest rising and falling with each breath. There was something about his words the other night that she couldn't shake. The way his voice had roughened as he spoke about walking away—he'd made a choice like that in his life, she was sure of it. It wasn't his profession, although the revelation that he hated it had been a surprise, too. There was a lot more to him than he let on, that much was for sure.

Henry shifted on the couch but didn't open his eyes, so she poured herself a cup of coffee and walked out onto the balcony.

The sun was rising behind her, and the city below was limned in gold. It was still cold, but it felt good, bracing. She wrapped her hands around her mug and remembered the warmth of the tea last night, the care he had taken with her.

What if I didn't have to do this? The idea was terrifying and freeing all at once. Maybe there was something out there that would fit her better, something that wouldn't keep weighing down on her like a piece of granite on her chest. But finding that, even *thinking* about it, was like looking at the sun. It hurt, and that hurt went deep.

But she couldn't stop contemplating it, like pressing on a bruise to see if it would still hurt the same way each time.

And at the same time, it felt like she could breathe finally. She was surfacing after a long time holding her breath, and the oxygen felt so good, so intoxicating, she couldn't get enough of it.

Behind her the door slid open, and without even turning around, she knew it was Henry. Ellie, even at her quietest, was too ebullient to move that silently. But Daphne still couldn't bring herself to look back at him, too afraid of what she'd see in his eyes. Probably not judgment, but perhaps pity, and that was even worse.

"You must be cold," he said, his voice pleasantly gravelly.

Daphne shrugged, her forearms propped on the railing. Henry approached, and something soft and warm brushed over her shoulders—the blanket he'd had on the couch. It felt good and smelled even better, like him. Daphne clutched it closed at her neck like a cape and risked a glance at him.

Henry was looking out over the city like she was, a mug of steaming coffee in his hands. He took a sip, saying nothing.

"Did you sleep okay? The couch couldn't have been very comfortable."

He huffed out a laugh. "Modern couches are exceptionally comfortable. I was quite all right."

"You didn't have to stay," she said, dragging her lower lip between her teeth.

Henry looked sideways at her. "On the contrary, my lady, I think I did."

"You haven't called me that in a while," Daphne said over the loud, insistent thumping of her heart.

"Yes, well, I thought it prudent."

"Why?"

Henry sipped his coffee without answering right away. "To remind myself."

He was sending clear warning signals, the signs practically flashing *stop pushing, let it go*, but she couldn't. "Of what?" The warmth of the blanket was melting into her, driving away a chill she hadn't noticed.

"Of how dangerous you are for me."

The words hung in the early-morning air. "Dangerous?" She tried to smile and play it off like a joke, but she couldn't. Her mouth was too dry, her throat too tight.

"Aye. Dangerous." His Scottish accent got thicker at times like this, moments when whatever it was between them started to take shape. He stole another look, one that dragged the remaining air from her lungs. "You know that."

"Do I?" she asked, and at his arched eyebrow, she shook her head. "I mean it. I'm not doing anything on purpose."

He huffed again, but he didn't sound amused. "It may not be on purpose, but that doesn't make it less dangerous to me."

"How?" She turned to face him and touched his forearm. He was in a T-shirt and his skin was chilled in the early-morning breeze, but it still scalded her palm. "Henry, I know—actually no, I don't know, but I think there's something here, between us. And I know it's different where you come from, but there's nothing wrong with us having feelings. Or—acting on them."

Henry's eyes flashed. "That's what you think this is about?"

"Um, yes?"

He shook his head and looked away. "I'm not that naive, Daphne." There it was again, her name on his lips, sending a shiver down her spine. "I'm a grown man. I understand what it is I'm feeling. And I've spent long enough here that I know things are different. That doesn't change anything."

"Why not? We're adults, and there's no shame in what we're feeling."

His throat bobbed as he swallowed. She was still touching him, and he'd gone still as a statue, but he wasn't moving away. "Because—being with you, Daphne, I can't come back from that. I cannot walk away, not when I'll have to, and I cannot leave my family alone and unprotected without me. They need me, but if I so much as kiss you, I won't be able to. I know that."

Desperate to lighten the mood, or at least shatter the tension a little, Daphne attempted to grin. "Are you so sure because you've time-traveled and kissed someone before?"

Henry's face stayed deadly serious, his eyes burning into her. He stepped closer and she had to tilt her chin up to keep looking at him. "No. But I have had my heart broken, and I know—I can't just kiss you, Daphne. It wouldn't be just that." He moved a lock of her hair back over her shoulder and his fingertips grazed the side of her neck. "You know that, and please don't—don't ask me to do something I can't."

"Okay," she said in a tiny voice she barely recognized. She had barely even let herself think about the possibility of being with Henry, but he shut the door so firmly there was no point in trying to imagine what might be behind it. "Thank you for taking care of me last night."

Henry looked impossibly sad. "Of course, my lady."

Chapter Twenty

There generally weren't any real "slow" shifts in the ER, but some were slower than others. Friday and Saturday nights tended to be a zoo, while midmorning during the week could be a little calmer. Some days, it was even calm enough for Daphne to sit down while eating her lunch, provided she didn't plan to be seated for more than fifteen minutes.

On one such morning, just a few days after her talk with Henry, Daphne found herself able to sit down and eat the sandwich he'd packed her—he had moved to elaborate sandwiches featuring a curry-mayo sauce combination that were, quite frankly, the best thing she'd ever eaten—and even have enough time to check her phone. None of her shifts had been as bad as the one that night, but it still felt like there was something unfinished hanging over her.

On a whim, she typed "how to change residencies" into her search bar, but the first post that came up was just information on how to get *into* a residency, which wasn't helpful, and anyway, even if she did leave her program, she had no idea what she'd want in a different one. She had liked her peds rotation well enough, but she couldn't handle the sadness of sick kids day in and day out. She liked the variety of the ER, the way she never quite knew what was coming; she just wanted more time, too. The next hit was a message board post from someone who had considered switching out of Emergency Medicine, and Daphne's pulse started to race as she clicked the link. But the post itself was just the person saying they had *thought* they hated Emergency Medicine but discovered that, actually, it was just a rough adjustment period and they learned to love it and didn't switch out after all.

Daphne's heart sank just as Vibol walked in. "What are you looking up?" he asked, dropping into the chair next to her.

"Nothing," she said, far too hastily. It felt like cheating, even considering switching programs. Their program director, Dr. Gupta, would be so disappointed, and Daphne couldn't bear disappointing her like that. She knew people switched—sometimes just to a different program to be closer to a spouse or family, sometimes because they weren't going to cut it in a super competitive field. Sometimes people switched because they hadn't matched into their first-choice field and the second-choice program wasn't a good fit.

But this was what Daphne had always wanted. She was in her first-choice program in her first-choice field, and leaving—no, she didn't want to. It was nice of Henry to be there for her when she needed him, but leaving her program wasn't the right way to fix things. Daphne had already gotten better at things since she started, so eventually—eventually—she'd fall in love with the job.

"How's Michelle?" Daphne said, sugar sweet.

Vibol narrowed his eyes. "She's good."

"How good?"

"None-of-your-damn-business good."

Daphne grinned, but before she could respond, Hannah stuck her head into the lounge. "We're about to get a bus accident. City bus versus a pickup. Everyone survived, but some are banged up. EMTs say there's nothing life threatening, but there were a bunch of high schoolers on the bus when it got hit, so it'll be a lot of freaked-out parents."

Vibol looked longingly at the sandwich he'd just pulled out—also a Henry-made specialty—and tossed it back into the fridge. "Guess we're back at it now."

◆ ◆ ◆

"How are you doing, Mariana?" Daphne said, pulling back the curtain to a bed. On the bed was a teenage girl—fifteen, according to the chart—with an ashen cast to her olive skin. As Hannah had predicted, the ER had been a flurry of activity since the first ambulance arrived, and she'd seen Mariana almost an hour ago, ordering an X-ray and some painkillers for what was almost certainly a broken tibia.

"Better, Dr. Griffin," she said quietly.

"Have you gotten a hold of your mom?"

Mariana nodded. "She had to talk to her boss, but he finally agreed to let her leave early."

"Then I'm sure she'll be here soon." Daphne pulled up the report from Radiology and nodded to herself. "Looks like you do have a fractured tibia, so you'll need a cast. But it doesn't need to be reset, which is really, really good news for you."

Mariana nodded again, but tears started leaking from the corners of her eyes.

"What's wrong? Are you still in pain?" Daphne asked. Mariana shook her head rapidly, the tears coming faster now.

Daphne had about ten more patients to see, but she grabbed the stool and sat down next to Mariana's bed. "Hey there, it's okay," she said gently. Mariana started reaching out, grasping at thin air, and Daphne let her take her hand. "It's okay, you're going to be okay," she murmured. "A broken leg sucks, but the cast won't be on for too long."

"It's—not that." Her patient hiccuped.

"Are you on a team? Is this going to mess up your season?" Daphne guessed. She wished she knew more about Mariana, so she could make her feel better without taking random stabs in the dark at what might be wrong.

"No, I'm just a nerd," Mariana said with a watery chuckle. "A broken leg won't stop me from being a Mathlete."

Daphne smiled encouragingly. "That's the spirit. It's going to be okay, I promise," she said, and squeezed her hand.

"I know, I'm just—it was so scary, and I feel—stupid. Nobody died, I'm fine, and I'm still so freaked out, and it's just so stupid."

"Being scared? Honey, you were in an accident that hurt a lot of people. That *is* scary. It would be weirder if you weren't freaked out, honestly."

That earned her another weak chuckle. "How long will the cast be on?"

"Six to eight weeks."

Mariana sniffed and sighed at the same time. "So I'll have it during prom, then."

"You've got a date already? Aren't you a sophomore?"

A blush started at Mariana's hairline. "My friend Grace said they wanted to go with me. But they haven't like, officially asked or anything, just mentioned it when we were hanging out last week."

"Well, if Grace is a good friend, they won't care if you've got a cast."

"I know, it just—"

"Sucks," Daphne finished. "And it does, you're right about that. But you could like, decorate the cast or something. Make it match your dress?"

"Mariana?" a voice called.

Mariana pushed herself up. "Mama?"

Daphne pulled back the curtain so Mariana's mother could make her way over. She teared up at the sight of her daughter, rushing over to wrap her in a tight hug. Daphne couldn't hear what she was saying, but both mother and daughter were sobbing, and she stepped back to give them some space.

After a few minutes Mariana's mother, Thea, straightened and wiped her cheeks dry. "Thank you for taking care of my baby," she said. "She says she broke her leg?"

Daphne ran Thea through what she'd told Mariana—the fracture, the cast, and the recovery. "It won't be fun, but within a few months, Mariana will be back to normal, I promise," she said. "The break isn't too bad, and with some physical therapy once the cast is off, she'll see no lasting effects."

"Thank you," Thea said again.

Daphne wanted to stay and keep talking, but she caught the eye of Dr. Gupta, who was talking to a teenage boy and a man who appeared to be his grandfather, and knew she'd lingered too long already. There were other patients to see, and with the orders in for Mariana's cast, there wasn't anything else she needed to do.

Daphne went to see her next patient—another bus rider, but this one a middle-aged woman with a sprained wrist—and shoved her wistfulness down.

An hour later, she walked past Vibol, who was hurrying out of his patient's bay, frowning at his phone.

"Hey, do you ever wish you had more time with people?"

He stopped reading his texts and looked at her, puzzled. "Like, in life?"

"No, I mean here. Don't you hate how rushed we are?"

"That's why we went into this, right? So we could patch people up and send them on to someone else? Of course I don't mind—it's what I like about it. I drop in, fix them, and then fly off like I'm Superman or some shit."

That wasn't how Daphne had felt after leaving Mariana, though. She'd felt like she was leaving with her job half done, and she didn't feel the euphoria she expected to, even when she'd done what she needed to at the best of her ability.

She chewed her lip, debating if it was worth telling Vibol how she felt, but he held up his phone. "You saw this, right?"

"No, what?" She pulled her phone out of her back pocket, realizing she'd missed nearly a dozen texts in the wild crush of bus patients. "What's happening?"

"Find the one from Ellie."

Daphne scrolled down, and her stomach jolted so hard she could have sworn it literally, physically moved.

ER Doc Group Chat

Ellie Levine

Fuck I misread the chart; Henry's portal opens TONIGHT not next week, and by tonight I mean SOON
I'm getting him ready and we're going now, I'm so sorry he can't say goodbye to anyone but it's this or waiting until the solstice, which is months away
Henry says "farewell"

Henry was leaving, and Daphne wasn't even going to get to say goodbye.

Chapter Twenty-One

Vibol checked his watch. "If you go now, you might catch them."

"Go? We've got an hour left on our shift."

"I'll cover for you. Go, Daph."

"But—"

Vibol held up his hand, an exasperated expression on his face. "Do you, or do you not, love him?"

"I—I can't—"

"Exactly. If you didn't, you'd say so. So fucking *go*, Daphne, now, before you miss your chance."

"What will I say? He's leaving."

"You're smart, you'll figure it out. Now go, before I stop being magnanimous and change my mind."

Daphne hesitated, her heart suddenly pounding. "I owe you!" she called, feet starting to move before her brain made the conscious decision.

"Big time," Vibol yelled after her.

Daphne grabbed her bike and started racing down the streets, feet pumping as hard as she could. She wasn't sure of the portal's exact location—Ellie had said it wasn't the same place as before, but she hadn't narrowed down the location, as far as Daphne knew—so the best place to start would be back at home. She'd just have to hope they hadn't left yet.

Daphne abandoned her bike, unlocked, at the rack and sprinted inside, not willing to even wait for the elevator. By the time she made it to their door, she was a disheveled, sweaty mess, but it would be worth it if she could see Henry and—

Well, she wasn't sure what she'd do or say. She couldn't keep him from leaving and wouldn't want to, but it felt strange for him to leave with so much left unsaid. She wasn't even sure how she'd phrase it, but she knew he needed to know how she felt, as clumsy and insufficient as her words might be.

But the apartment was silent. The tears sprang into her eyes as she closed the door behind her, wondering if it was even worth texting Ellie to find out where they were. It sounded like she and Henry had been rushing, so perhaps there wasn't any point.

A folded piece of paper lay on the table, and Daphne forced herself to pick it up. She knew what it was before she even opened it, and part of her didn't want to read it, because a goodbye from Henry would be too final to bear. But Daphne hadn't gotten this far in life by shying away from hard things, so she opened it and read through tear-blurred eyes.

> Dearest Daphne,
>
> I'm not sure if I'll ever get the courage to give you this, but I am afraid our days together are drawing to a close, and I don't believe I'll ever quite work up the nerve to tell you this directly, either. Which leaves the written word, and this has never been my forte. For that I apologize, but leaving without telling you the truth seems far worse than exposing you to my inelegant phrasing.
>
> First, an explanation for my reticence on the balcony that morning. Not kissing you may be one of my life's greatest regrets, and indeed it is already the thing I wish I could change between us. But I've had my heart broken before, and I knew that if I kissed you, it would shatter.

When I was still at university, I fell in love with a woman far above my station, the daughter of a duke. I know you'll likely scoff at that, and I understand, as after living here for this time, I understand why it seems absurd. But where I am from, it doesn't matter how wealthy one is—if you're not from the aristocracy, there are limits to how far you can rise. I had naively thought my father's wealth might be enough, but it wasn't. I went to offer for her hand in marriage, and her father laughed at me.

A year later she was married to someone else, and I swore I would never risk a heartbreak like that again. That was an easy promise to keep until I met you, Miss Griffin. I've never felt this way before, and I know I never will again. More than anything, that morning on the balcony, I wanted you to ask me to stay. I know I cannot, but I wanted it all the same, and that breaks my heart more than you'll ever know. You've wounded me so deeply, I fear I shall never recover. I do not tell you this to hurt you, but so you know, if I am gone, that the feelings I suspect you have were returned, but that it was for fear of breaking us both that I refrained.

I also suspect you will find that unbearably patriarchal of me, and for that I do beg your forgiveness. It may not have been my decision to make for you, but my cowardice won out. Please forgive me for that, and for letting you doubt I felt the same. I love you, Daphne, and I suspect I always will.

Forever yours,
Henry MacDonald

The world spun around her. Henry loved her, and he was gone. Forever.

It was almost impossible to comprehend, harder to get her brain around than the fact that she had gone and fallen for the asshole in the first place. He didn't fit into her life plan—although to be fair, time travel in general wasn't something that would fit neatly anywhere—but now that he was gone, she knew it would be nearly impossible to recover. Henry had kept his distance to protect them both, but it had been pointless. She couldn't keep her heart safe from him, and now there was nothing to do but grieve.

She looked around her and Ellie's apartment, hoping for another trace of him, but there was nothing. The pantry and fridge were probably stocked, since he'd recently started braving the grocery store with Brittany, but that was it. No other sign of the man who had quite literally dropped into her life out of nowhere, only to reorient it completely.

Daphne blinked, the tears starting to track down her cheeks. The doorknob twisted and she straightened, not wanting Ellie to immediately notice her devastation.

But then the door swung open. Henry strode through the door, tossing a backpack aside and catching her face in his hands before she even quite registered this was real, and not a hallucination. "I couldn't," he growled, and then he kissed her.

His lips were soft, but his jaw was rough, the stubble he must not have had time to shave prickling under her fingers. Daphne's brain finally caught up, and she found herself kissing him back just as hard and desperately. He smelled like the outdoors, like fresh air and grass, and she tunneled her fingers into his hair to hold him close as he wrapped his arms around her waist.

"I couldn't leave," he murmured against her lips when they broke for air. "Not without kissing you."

Daphne sought his lips for a slower, softer kiss. "When does the portal open?" All Ellie's text had said was that it was soon. Maybe it wasn't open yet, and this was just a goodbye.

"It's closed," Ellie said smugly.

Daphne pulled away from Henry to peer over his shoulder. "What? Henry, you didn't go?"

"I didn't," he confirmed, cuffing his hand around the back of her neck to kiss her again.

"But—your family."

Something sad flickered behind his eyes. "I'll return to them eventually."

"Oh good, they're finally acting on it," Michelle said, and Daphne had to pull away again. Michelle was next to Ellie, on her tiptoes.

"Wait, so he didn't leave?" Brittany was behind her, arms crossed, wearing an identical smug expression to Ellie's.

"He didn't. He's staying until the solstice."

"Can you guys leave?" Daphne said, the grin on her face at complete odds with her irritated tone.

"Depends. How much of a show are we going to get? And did Ellie buy popcorn?" Brittany asked.

"I bought groceries this week, and no, I did not," Henry said, walking purposefully over to the door. "Daphne will text when we're ready to talk to everyone." He shooed them out and shut the door firmly.

"This is my apartment, you know," Ellie called through the door.

"Go hang out with someone else for an hour and then come back."

"Okay, but don't have sex on the countertops, please. I don't want to eat where you've fucked."

"Noted. Now go away," Daphne yelled, doing a bad job of stifling her giggles. She half expected Henry to look scandalized, but he was chuckling, too. She turned and he tugged her in for a kiss, this time with a little less urgency but no less need.

"You really stayed for me?" she asked.

Henry kept his forehead against hers and tucked a lock of her hair behind her ear. "I did," he whispered.

"I got your letter. I'm sorry about your ex."

Henry gave her a small, sad smile and moved back, enough to look her in the eye but still close enough to keep his hands on her waist. "I was very young. I won't say it was for the best, but I suspect it would have been a difficult marriage if I'd gotten my way. But it left a deep impression that was hard to shake."

Daphne touched his cheek, and he nuzzled her palm. "You're going back, though?"

"Ellie said the portal is opening again in a few months. I'll go then."

The solstice. That was barely three months away, but it was more than she thought she'd get with him, so she would take it. "Is it . . . opening after that?"

Henry's face was etched with pain. "Not for another seven years."

Three months, then. That was all they would have. "Thank you for staying," she said, taking his hand. "And for what you said in your letter."

"I felt so foolish leaving it," he admitted, and tugged her close for a hug. She rested her temple against his cheek. "Part of me worried I'd misread you."

"But you stayed anyway?"

She felt, rather than saw, him smile. "I judged it would be worse to miss this time with you no matter what. I'd rather have been wrong and be stuck here for a few more very awkward months than risk losing you entirely."

Daphne kissed him, and slowly the kiss started to shift, from jubilant to needy, from gentle to something deeper, hungrier. Henry walked her backward to her bedroom door, his lips never leaving hers. She tugged at his shirt while he kicked the door shut. He breathed out shakily, and she took a half step back. "Sorry, I—there's a part of me that feels I'm ruining you," he said with a wry smile.

"Does it help if I say I've already been ruined?"

He huffed out a laugh. "Not really, no," he said, but he tenderly tucked a lock of hair back behind her ear. "I just—I needed a moment, that's all. Your world takes some adjusting." Henry pulled her back to him, finding her lips with his.

"Are you sure?" she gasped.

Henry dragged his lips down the curve of her jaw, finding the soft hollow behind her ear. "Aye," he growled. "Never been more sure in my life."

She softly cursed his nineteenth-century clothes—the buttons did not slide as easily as she was used to—and he chuckled, placing his hands over hers. "Like this," he said, and together they undid his shirt buttons so she could shove the shirt back over his shoulders. Henry pulled the T-shirt she had on up over her head with much less fanfare.

Slowly, piece by piece, they shed their clothes. They stumbled together in the direction of her mattress, ending up with Daphne on top when Henry fell backward onto the bed. She giggled and he silenced her with a kiss that went on so long she stopped thinking, stopped breathing, stopped being anything other than a bundle of nerves and urges, desire overriding all higher-level thought.

Henry wasn't gone. He loved her, and he was staying. *Only for a little while,* a nasty voice whispered deep in the recesses of her brain, but she silenced it.

He pulled her down, her chest on top of his, and curled his hand gently around the back of her neck to keep her close. Leisurely they explored each other's mouths, taking time she had thought they'd never have. He dipped his chin down to trace the swell of her breast with the tip of his tongue and she arched against him, grinding her core against his pelvis. She was slick already, swollen with need, and Henry made a strangled noise deep in his throat.

"You'll be the death of me," he panted, and Daphne couldn't help it. She smirked and started walking on her knees higher, pausing to arch her brow down at him.

Henry hesitated, but ran his palms up the outsides of her thighs, never breaking their gaze. He nodded and she began moving again, settling herself above him with a knee on either side of his head.

"Fuck," he growled. "The twenty-first century really is an age of miracles."

Daphne giggled again, but then he wrapped his palms around her hips and pulled her onto his mouth, and the laugh died in her throat. Instead she keened, bracing herself on the headboard. Henry licked from her entrance to her clit, and she buried her face in her biceps, trying in vain to stifle the groan he wrenched from her. She felt his lips curl into a smile even as he teased her clit, lashing it mercilessly back and forth while heat coiled in her belly and sparks flew along her nerve endings. Daphne ground herself against his chin and *felt* his groan in her core. Her thighs were trembling and his fingertips dug in, steadying her against his mouth. Henry licked at her entrance and she almost bent in half, gasping for air that refused to fill her lungs, and then one more flick of his tongue against her clit had her falling, shivering and unraveling while just his hands on her thighs held her up.

She fell, boneless, to the bed, and Henry helped her arrange her now-useless limbs with a grin that reminded her of how irritating she used to find him. He was arrogant, that was for sure, but she could let it slide because, *damn*, he knew what he was doing. Henry kissed her, softly brushing her hair back while he let her taste herself on his lips. She turned and stretched languidly to dig a condom out of her bedside stand but then paused when she had it open, realizing she knew next to nothing about contraception in the 1880s. "Do you . . . know what this is?" she asked, way too shyly for someone who had just been sitting on his face.

Henry peered at it. "Is that a french letter?"

Daphne shrugged and laughed. "No idea. How about I explain what it does, and we go from there?"

Henry laughed too, leaning over for one more kiss between their smiles. "By all means. Explain."

Daphne did her best two-minute-sex-ed explanation of condoms, and he agreed that it was, in fact, a french letter, and thus he was aware of what it did. She helped him roll it on, and he urged her shoulders back down to the mattress, covering her with his bulk.

When Henry slid inside her, she had to close her eyes. It was too perfect, too much. He nipped gently at her chin and nuzzled her cheek until she opened them, and then he punished her by pulling almost all the way out and gliding back in, the stretch achingly, shiveringly perfect.

Daphne wrapped her arms around his neck to hold him close and let him tilt her hips up, his rhythm at once too slow and too much, turning her muscles to liquid and her thoughts to mere fragments. She didn't think it was possible after coming so recently, but soon she was climbing the peak again, the pressure building and ratcheting higher and higher with each thrust of his hips.

And then, suddenly, the wave crested and she came, biting his shoulder to keep from screaming herself hoarse. Henry's hips stuttered, the rhythm faltering, and then a few strokes later, he came too, spilling into the condom with a hoarse groan.

"I love you, Dr. Daphne Griffin," he murmured into her ear, both of them still panting, desperate for air.

"I love you too, Henry MacDonald," she whispered back.

Chapter Twenty-Two

Daphne stood in the kitchen, teaching Henry the joys of eating peanut butter straight from the jar, when there was a knock at the door. "Can I come home now?" Ellie called plaintively.

"It's safe." Daphne giggled and hid her face in Henry's shoulder.

"Oh thank god, you're both dressed," Ellie said.

"Whatever else would we be wearing?" Henry asked.

"You obviously haven't paid enough attention to the postcoital scenes in rom-coms." Ellie clucked. "She should be wearing your shirt and nothing else."

Henry raised his eyebrows at Daphne, making her break out into giggles again. Daphne wasn't much of a giggler, except, it would seem, when it came to Henry. "Perhaps we shall wait for you to have a night shift, then, because I like the sound of that."

"As long as I don't have to see it." Ellie stuck her head back out the door. "It's safe, guys," she announced.

"Oh thank god," Brittany said, holding the door for Vibol and Michelle.

"I ask again, is this a communal apartment?" Henry muttered.

"It is, yeah," Vibol replied.

"So are you staying for good?" Michelle asked.

Henry tossed Daphne a sad look. "I cannot, no. When the solstice arrives, I'll have to leave."

"When does the portal open again after that?" Vibol asked. "It's a while, right?"

"Seven years," Daphne said, and had to clear her throat.

Vibol whistled low. "Then we'll have to make it a kickass few months, won't we?"

Henry wrapped his arm around Daphne's waist and tugged her closer. "What did you have in mind?"

◆ ◆ ◆

Daphne held the bike steady while Henry fiddled with the buckle on his helmet. "Is this really necessary?" he asked, pointing to the helmet.

It did, admittedly, look dorky as hell. But Daphne was an emergency department doctor, and that meant she'd seen more head injuries in the last eight months than she cared to count. "Yes, very much so," she said. "Now hop on."

Henry looked dubious but did as she instructed. They had practiced in the gym in their building's basement on an exercise bike so he could get a feel for it, but now they were on an empty basketball court at a park in the middle of downtown, not too far from where she'd first run him over—on that very bike. "It's just like how you practiced, except now you have to balance. The faster you go, the easier it will be."

"How can I go fast if it's standing still?"

"I'll hold on and push to get you started," Daphne said. "And if you feel like you're going to fall, just jump off. It's just like riding a horse."

"Is it?" Henry asked, cocking his head.

"I assume so. I've never done it."

Henry grinned. "Then perhaps that's the next thing we shall try." He leaned over and brushed a kiss to her cheek, quick and thoughtless, and she wished she could have this forever. It was so easy with him, so of course it would have an end date.

Henry placed his feet on the pedals and gave her an uneasy nod, accompanied by a crooked grin as she pushed the bike by the seat and started jogging. Henry pedaled just as they had practiced, so Daphne let go and stopped running, only to see him wobble and fall over a mere five feet in front of her.

He had tried to do what she'd instructed—let the bike crash and jump off—but he got tangled and went down on the pavement with a very undignified grunt. Daphne hurried over to help, picking the bike up while Henry inspected his arms and legs. "Nothing's bleeding," he observed. "But that was a bit harder than riding a horse, you know."

Daphne held out her hand to pull him up. "Let's try again."

Henry managed to keep the bike going straight without toppling over at least four times before they called it quits. He still couldn't turn very well, and braking was hit or miss, but he was getting there. "What about you?" he asked as they walked her bike back to the building.

"Already know how to ride a bike, thanks."

He snorted. "I meant, what would you want to do? I wanted to learn how to ride a bike, but while I'm here, what do you want to do?" He faltered slightly on *here*, as did her heart.

"Promise not to laugh?"

"Promise," he vowed seriously.

"I want to go on a date. A real date, where we get dressed up and go somewhere nice to eat and split a bottle of wine." She looked down and away, wondering why the admission was making her blush.

"Why would that make me laugh?" Henry asked.

"It's just—cheesy. Corny. Outdated."

"Is it what you want?"

"It is," Daphne said.

"Then where do you want to eat?"

◆ ◆ ◆

Daphne clasped the necklace her parents had gotten her as a med school graduation present around her neck and stepped back, her stomach oddly fluttery. They had reservations at a restaurant in the Warehouse

District, a new place by some up-and-coming chefs that featured the kitchen in the center, so Henry would be able to watch how they prepared food. Given his obsession with cooking shows, she thought he might like that, and she'd been wanting to try it but hadn't had an excuse for dropping quite that much money on one dinner before now.

The restaurant itself wasn't overtly fancy, but since this was her fancy date night, dammit, Daphne had gone for a simple black dress and heels. Dressy but not fussy. She forced herself to stop smoothing her hair back and adjusting the neckline of her dress and just go out into the living room, where Henry and Vibol were bickering over the correct way to tie a tie.

"Hey, Daph," Vibol said with a half glance her way. "Your man's almost ready, if he would just. Stop. Fidgeting."

Henry glanced her way and went abruptly still. Slowly he turned to face her, his eyes dragging up and down her body in a way she could almost *feel.* The tips of his ears turned red, and she bit her lip, absurdly pleased that even after they'd slept together, he could get flustered just looking at her. "Are you ready, my lady?" he asked formally, after the silence between them had drawn out long enough that Vibol appeared ready to snap.

"Ready," she confirmed, and took his offered arm. There might not be much time for them, but she'd be damned if she wasted a second.

◆ ◆ ◆

Henry eyed the wine list carefully, a vaguely amused look on his face, before ordering a bottle for them to split. Henry had been enthralled when they arrived, delighted to be able to watch the chefs at work, and had torn his eyes away from them only when it was time to choose the wine. He had done a hilarious double take when he first saw the prices, although he had since recovered, mostly because Daphne had assured him she could afford it. When the server was safely out of earshot, Daphne raised her eyebrows. "What's so funny?"

Henry shrugged. "All the dates for the wine are in the past from now, but sometimes it still feels like those years are in the future."

Daphne considered that. It had seemed like Henry had adapted to the twenty-first century very seamlessly by now, but he was still a man out of time. "What's it like, though? The past?"

The server returned with the bottle, and they both leaned back, waiting until she'd departed again. "Quieter," he said thoughtfully. "And darker, although the night sky is brighter. Getting dressed is far more involved, especially for women, and the clothing is a lot less comfortable."

"But what's it like for you? What do you miss?"

"My family, of course. And George." Henry took a sip of wine, playing with the stem of the glass. "There's fewer demands on your attention there. Makes it easier to be absorbed in work, although harder to be informed. You have so many choices here, so many options when it comes to everything, that I think it's easy to be overwhelmed, while back home everything is just—quieter. Not necessarily simpler, but quieter."

"You make it sound lovely," Daphne said.

"It is—was," Henry corrected himself. "In some ways. In others, I'm not so sure. People's lives are freer now, less constricted. Not just women, either. I feel more like myself here, and I don't think I ever really thought about it that way back then. My sisters would be happier here, and George, too. Maybe even my mother, although it's hard to imagine her in something like jeans."

"Have you ever thought about seeing what their lives were like? Looking into it?" Daphne asked. The server set their plates down, and they tucked into their first course.

"I talked about it with Ellie once. But she thought because I'm planning to go back, it wouldn't be a good idea. Might screw things up, somehow." He didn't look up at her while speaking, and once again the specter of his departure appeared between them.

Daphne swallowed over the lump in her throat. "What's something you're looking forward to? When you go back?"

Henry paused, gazing over at the open kitchen for long enough that Daphne wondered if he hadn't heard her question. "The feel of the fireplace in the evening. Modern heating is marvelous, don't get me wrong, but I miss spending evenings reading in front of the fireplace with my mother and Annie and Mags, hearing the hiss and crackle of logs and feeling the heat when I approach the hearth."

Part of Daphne wanted to protest that he could experience that in the twenty-first century, that they had fireplaces here, too. But she knew that wasn't really what he missed; he missed his family, the feeling of comfort that came from being *home*. She couldn't blame him for that and knew she would probably miss something equally quotidian, if she had accidentally fallen through a time portal. Probably just sitting around with Ellie on a quiet morning, drinking coffee and doing a crossword puzzle. Nothing that on the surface couldn't be replicated elsewhere, but would never feel the same without Ellie.

"I'm sorry, I've made you sad," Henry said. "I didn't mean to. This is supposed to be a date, and I'm given to understand these should be light and fun."

"They're whatever they need to be," Daphne said, and then did something that she never would have thought she'd do. She stood up and walked around the edge of the table, bending down and kissing him solidly. A few tables around them broke into scattered claps and nervous giggles, and Daphne straightened, smiling down at him. "I love you, Henry. No matter what."

Henry tangled his fingers with hers, pressing a soft kiss to the back of her hand. "I love you too, Daphne. Always."

Chapter Twenty-Three

"And you trust this man?" Henry asked for the hundredth time.

Brittany shrugged. "My cousin said he's not like, a murderer or anything."

"I am less concerned about his character than his abilities," Henry said darkly.

"Oh, she said he's a super good pilot."

"Super good," Henry echoed disbelievingly.

Daphne squeezed his hand. "We don't need to do this," she offered.

"But according to you, without identification I cannot get on a larger aeroplane, and in order to get that, I would need to commit, and I quote, 'several federal crimes, probably,' so if I *want* to experience the wonder of flight, this is my only option."

"*Airplane*, not *aeroplane*," Daphne interjected.

"I'll call it what I damn well please, woman," Henry grumbled.

"My cousin is totally trustworthy," Brittany promised. "Just because she dumped him doesn't mean he's bad at his job."

In front of them, the small plane Brittany's cousin's ex-boyfriend owned puttered to a stop. "You must be Brittany," he said, standing in front of them on the tarmac. "I'm Chad. Who all is going up?"

"All three of us," she explained.

"And you must be the friend with the interesting background," Chad said with his hands on his hips. They had told him Henry was from an off-the-grid commune and hadn't had much experience with the world. When Chad had suggested to Brittany that perhaps a commercial flight would be a little less intense for him, Brittany had had to come up with an explanation for his lack of ID on the spot. *His parents didn't believe in filing government paperwork, so he doesn't have a birth certificate or anything,* she had said.

"That would be me."

Chad straightened the blue baseball hat on his head and nodded toward the single-engine plane. "You ready?"

Henry tightened his grip on Daphne's hand, but his face didn't show any apprehension. "I am indeed."

As it turned out, single-engine airplanes were *loud*. Their headsets allowed them to talk, but Henry appeared taken aback by the noise even before they began taxiing toward the runway. He was quieter than usual, and as the plane began accelerating, Daphne heard a sibilant hiss as he inhaled sharply. His jaw was tight, a muscle twitching, and Daphne wished she could sit next to him, rather than behind Chad.

But then the wheels left the ground, and his face transformed. He went from tense and anxious to staring around, agape at the world. There wasn't much to see, no mountains or oceans or even any of the Great Lakes, just cornfields and small blue-green ponds dotting the countryside, with the Minneapolis skyline off in the distance.

But the sky was crystal clear, a bright, almost-summery blue, and the fields were a promising spring green. And the smile on Henry's face was brighter than the sun.

He looked around in awe, too absorbed in what he saw to even speak. When they landed he helped open the door and held out his hand, first to Brittany and then to Daphne. For a split second, Daphne wondered if this was what it would be like if she lived in the past with him: Henry holding his hand out to help her down from a horse-drawn carriage. She wondered if he saw it too, a flash of what their lives could be like together, because for a moment he looked sad. But then he brightened and kissed her cheek, thanking her for showing him *a wonder I never even dreamed of seeing.*

But his smile was thanks enough.

◆ ◆ ◆

Daphne had never been this happy. Not when she got into her first-choice medical school, or matched with her dream residency program. She had always vaguely assumed having a boyfriend of some sort would be a net-neutral move, with the added joy of having a partner being somewhat canceled out by that partner finding her too serious or too committed to her job.

But Henry didn't seem bothered by any of it. He had decamped from Helen's, on account of her returning soon from Florida, and after a brief, only-slightly-awkward conversation about propriety, norms, and morals, moved into Daphne's room. He knew she would sometimes have to work overnight, and on those days, he cheerfully did any sort of housework she and Ellie had fallen behind on and spent his time either trying to learn more about the world or perfecting his cooking.

And really, he was getting to be very good. With Michelle's help, he had created a bucket list of food he wanted to make while he had access to modern cooking equipment and was methodically working his way through the list, starting with South Asia. It meant every day for Daphne started in Henry's arms and ended with her eating something delicious, and she was practically floating.

Everything was perfect, except for the one big thing that wasn't. Daphne's heart wasn't in her work, and people were starting to notice. Dr. Gupta had even pulled her aside for a chat after a particularly rough set of rounds.

"What's wrong, Daphne?" Dr. Gupta had asked, her face creased with concern. Daphne had panicked, worried she'd screwed up, and quickly reviewed everything she'd said during rounds, but nothing stuck out to her as a glaring error. That panicked her even more, until Dr. Gupta held up her hand. "You're not in trouble; I'm just worried. You don't seem like yourself lately. Is everything okay?"

"I—uh—yeah, I'm okay," Daphne stammered. Ellie and Vibol walked past her and bugged their eyes out at her, which definitely didn't help. "I'm sorry if I screwed something up."

"You didn't, and I think you know you didn't," she said kindly. "But lately I've been feeling like you're, how should I put it, less than committed to this residency."

I want to quit. The words floated to the tip of her tongue, and she just barely managed to snatch them back. Daphne fought against her instinct to smooth it all away, however, and settled for something approaching the truth. "I've been struggling," she admitted. "It's overwhelming sometimes."

"Of course it is, but you're a bright student and a good doctor," Dr. Gupta reassured her. "But this is what we signed up for when we decided on emergency medicine, so whatever it is that's bothering you, part of our job as doctors is to figure it out and put it aside for the duration of your shift. Understood?"

"Understood, Dr. Gupta," Daphne confirmed.

Vibol and Ellie cornered her as Dr. Gupta walked away, both of them looking anxious.

"You didn't get in trouble, did you?" Ellie asked.

"I'd find that hard to believe would happen with Dr. Perfect here. But what did she want? Looked serious," Vibol said.

"She wanted to know why I was distracted lately."

"Did you tell her it's because you're finally getting laid?" Ellie asked.

Daphne elbowed her. "No, of course not."

But rather than join in the ribbing, Vibol looked at her thoughtfully. "She's right, though."

"That Daphne needed to get laid more often before this? Or that we can tell she's finally getting laid?"

"No, that she's distracted. Something's changed, hasn't it? And not just Henry. Something here, at the hospital."

"No, it's not that," Daphne said.

"But it's something, isn't it?" Vibol pushed.

"It's nothing," Daphne insisted. "Besides, we need to get back to work," she added, hoping neither would notice the distraction. "Hannah's giving us a dirty look."

Hannah was doing nothing of the sort, but Daphne slandered her anyway, just to get out of the conversation. If Vibol knew something was wrong, he'd start pushing her on it. Ellie didn't seem to have caught on, which wasn't like her, but maybe she really was attributing it to a new-relationship glow with Henry.

Daphne might be able to tell them it was the bittersweetness of knowing Henry had stayed for her with the knowledge that he was leaving in just a few short months, but that would only work short-term. Because Daphne was rapidly realizing that staying in emergency medicine long-term might not be possible, not if she was already losing interest.

But that meant opening a whole separate can of worms, and she wasn't quite ready to do that.

◆ ◆ ◆

"Are you ready?" Vibol asked.

"Ready," Henry confirmed.

"Do you need Daphne to hold your hand?" Ellie asked.

"When I was thirteen, I broke my wrist, and I survived just fine."

Daphne laughed. "Yeah, but didn't you get opium for that?"

"Medicinally."

"Exactly. That is a lot stronger than what we usually give now, so not the best comparison."

"Just how painful are these vaccines going to be?"

Vibol pulled the stash out of the cart. He'd managed to wheedle a series of vaccines that were about to expire from the hospital pharmacist, and now Henry was sequestered in a room in the ER on a slow Monday afternoon. "I'm just messing with you—they don't hurt at all," he said.

Daphne motioned for Henry to roll up his shirtsleeve and bare his biceps. "What's in that one?" Henry asked.

"Measles, mumps, and rubella. I know you said you already had measles, but they don't really sell the *M* and *R* parts of the MMR vaccine separately," Daphne explained.

Ellie finished cleaning the skin and stepped back, nodding to Vibol like they were surgeons in an operating room. "Patient is prepped and ready, Dr. Law."

"Thank you, Dr. Levine," he replied, and jabbed Henry in the arm.

Henry winced. "You said that wouldn't hurt at all," he accused Vibol.

"I lied." He shrugged. "Next up: polio."

Henry glared at him and then turned back to Daphne. "You said most of these are diseases that children catch, correct? Then why give them to me?"

"For one thing, they're diseases that are most deadly *for* children, not that adults don't ever get them. So it'll protect you from that. For another, it'll make it less likely for you to give it to a child." She bit the inside of her cheek, doing her best not to think about the fact that Henry might one day go on to have children with someone else. She wanted him to be happy, she really did, but she couldn't pretend that image didn't hurt a little.

Henry winced again as the needle went in, and Daphne switched sides so Vibol could put the remaining ones in his left arm. "And these have truly been so successful you've never even seen some of these?"

"I saw measles once," Ellie said, tossing the alcohol wipe. "Had a case in here my second shift. But never polio, or the others."

"It's been so successful people don't remember these diseases kill kids," Vibol grumbled. He placed a Band-Aid over Henry's injection site. "Flu shot is something we do annually, so this one won't last. The others all last longer, so long as we can get you at least one more before you leave."

"It won't be the full schedule, but it's better than nothing," Daphne agreed, ignoring the way her heart started to curl in on itself at the thought of him leaving. *He's not leaving yet, we still have time,* she reminded herself.

"Will these make me sick?" he asked.

"You'll probably feel like shit tonight, yeah," Ellie said. "But I planned ahead and bought instant ramen for you."

Henry brightened. "The Japanese dish? I've been meaning to try that."

"The real thing is better," Vibol warned. "The instant stuff is mostly salt, but yeah, it'll be what you want in about"—he glanced at the clock—"six to twelve hours."

"We'll stay in and watch a movie tonight," Daphne said.

Vibol and Ellie trashed their gloves and exchanged a look. "Glad I'm working tonight," Ellie said, making a face.

"Speaking of, if we're not down in the ED in five, Gupta will probably kill us," Vibol said. "You're welcome for the continual protection from disease and the miracle of modern medicine."

"Thank you," Henry said, laughing but sincere. He took Daphne's hand in his and turned to her. "Now, about that ramen."

Chapter Twenty-Four

Daphne was still in her room, tugging the dress into place. The annual hospital gala was about wining and dining donors for the attendings, but for residents like them, it was really an excuse to dress up and drink while someone else paid the bill. Henry had been delighted at the idea, since those sorts of events were apparently the main form of entertainment for wealthier people back in his day. Henry and Ellie had had a long, in-depth conversation about exactly how "rich merchant in Edinburgh" stacked up against Ellie's vast knowledge of the English Regency, courtesy of her extensive romance novel collection. It would seem there were a lot of similarities (he did go to balls, and he knew how to dance, as was expected of a man of his age) but also some differences (mainly that he didn't spend a lot of time in London, and also he lived about seventy years after most of those books were set and considered a lot of Ellie's understandings to be "rather dated").

"Are y'all ready?" Brittany called, opening their front door. "Because the RideShare is on its way, so you better be."

"Stop stalling and get out here," Ellie yelled through Daphne's door. There wasn't really a reason for her to feel so nervous, but still butterflies ricocheted through her chest and made her hands tremble like they did the first time she'd had to intubate a patient. But if the car was on its way, there really wasn't much else she could do.

Daphne squared her shoulders and walked out to an explosion of noise. "Jesus Christ, that is not fair," Ellie yelled. "Why the fuck are you so pretty?"

"Holy shit," Brittany exclaimed at the same time. "What god did you sacrifice to, and can I do that, too?"

But Daphne's gaze went straight toward Henry, who was looking at her with such softness she had to turn away. "Thanks, guys," she muttered. "Where's Vibol and Michelle?"

"They're meeting us downstairs. You ready?" Brittany said.

"You look lovely," Henry murmured and tucked Daphne's hand into the crook of his arm. He was in a borrowed suit from Vibol that stretched nicely across his shoulders, and a blush crawled up Daphne's chest from the deep neckline of her dark-blue dress.

"Gross," Ellie said, grinning. "Like, happy for you guys and all, but also: gross."

"Gross indeed," Brittany sighed.

Vibol and Michelle were in fact waiting in the lobby, and his tie was a light purple that matched her dress. "Aren't you going to make fun of them, too?" Daphne grumbled to Ellie.

"Already did," Ellie said, with an inexplicable high five to Vibol.

◆ ◆ ◆

A thing that none of them had considered, despite being five of the most overeducated people around and a time traveler, was that some people from the hospital might recognize Henry. Meghan was the first to clock him, even though she hadn't spent much time with him.

"Isn't he the 'I'm from the past' guy?" she asked them as they stood around with glasses of wine. Henry was off at the bar, having said he wanted to "brave the crowds" and "explore what this century had to offer for refreshment."

"He's my cousin," Michelle blurted, and then immediately shot the rest of them an *oops* face when Meghan looked understandably confused, given Michelle's being Black and Henry's being very much not. "Uh, second cousin," she amended. "He was here visiting me when the, um, accident happened?"

"Are you asking me or telling me?" Meghan replied.

"Uh, telling," Michelle said, and sent another frantic look at them when Meghan turned to place her wine on the empty table behind them.

"She didn't know him before this trip," Vibol explained. "Distant family, visiting some cousins—she had no idea who he was until the next weekend, once the whole, um, past thing had been sorted out."

Henry approached and Daphne watched in horror as Ellie tried to signal him with the neck-slicing "don't say anything" motion. He clearly didn't understand, and Daphne couldn't blame him. He wouldn't recognize Meghan, given how disorienting that first day had been and how briefly they'd interacted, and anyway, he would have no way of knowing what they were talking about.

So of course, he opened with the worst possible sentence: "This century has marvelous—"

"Hahaha, such a joker, this one," Vibol said loudly. "We were just explaining to Meghan here about how you're Michelle's cousin, but your accident had made your identification kind of difficult to track down, right?"

"Oh yes, ah, exceedingly so," Henry said, with a quick furrowed-brow look at Daphne. "Michelle and I are—cousins?"

"Second cousins," Michelle repeated.

"Oh hey, there's that, uh, person we wanted to talk to," Brittany said, pointing wildly. "Let's go over there. Now."

Daphne tugged a bewildered Henry behind them and out into the hall. "That was a close one," Ellie sighed dramatically.

"I don't know about you guys, but I'm not sure she bought that," Vibol said with a glance back into the ballroom.

Henry looked carefully at Michelle. "Will she believe we're cousins? I don't mean to be indelicate, but won't she notice that we're, well—"

"That I'm Black and you're white? Yeah, she'll notice. But, you know, families can be big and weird, so hopefully she'll just assume I've got some white relatives or something."

"I'll be honest, I think the bigger problem is that we were all just incredibly weird back there," Ellie observed. "Like, turbo weird."

"Possibly the weirdest we've ever been," Brittany agreed.

"We probably created more problems than we solved there, but at least Michelle was quick enough to come up with something on the spot."

"Should I go do damage control?" Daphne asked.

"Genuinely don't think that's possible, especially not with you. No offense," Ellie said and grinned at her. Daphne smiled back ruefully, taking Ellie's point. Improv had never been her strong suit.

Vibol shrugged. "Probably best if we just keep on going like nothing happened. The more we try to explain, the harder it gets. He's Michelle's cousin—"

"Second cousin," Michelle interjected.

Vibol nodded. "He's her second cousin, and when Daphne cruelly rode him down with her bike—"

"Hey, objection," Daphne protested.

"Overruled," Vibol said, holding up his hand. "She rode him down, gave him a teeny-tiny brain injury that temporarily made him believe he was from a different century, because he was on his way home from a *Bridgerton* reenactment and happened to be wearing that costume. End of story."

"Won't they notice my clothes are some seventy-odd years more modern than that?" Henry asked.

"Nope," everyone said in unison.

"What shall we do next?" he asked.

"You guys should go dance," Ellie said with a gesture at Vibol, Michelle, Daphne, and Henry. "Leave me and Brittany to go on the prowl."

◆ ◆ ◆

Daphne smiled as Vibol joined her at their table, Ellie walked onto the dance floor with Henry, and Michelle headed toward the restroom. Brittany was deep in conversation with Dr. Gupta and an older white man in a tuxedo over in the corner.

Vibol leaned back into his chair, jacket tossed on the empty seat next to him. "So what is your deal?" he asked.

Daphne was busy studying Henry and the figure he cut in his suit, and didn't quite pick up on the undercurrent in Vibol's tone. "Hmm?"

"Your deal," he repeated. "Something's up with you."

"Just a bad few weeks at work," she said dismissively.

"Nope, it's not that," he replied.

"And how do you know that for sure?"

"I can tell. Come on, Daph, give me some credit. I'm smart and I know you well."

"Not that well," she said acidly. Her stomach was suddenly roiling.

"Want to know what I think it is?" he asked, undeterred by her coldness.

"Why do I get the sense you're telling me no matter what?"

He shot her a cocky grin. "See? We know each other well." He laced his fingers together and rested his elbows on the table. "I think you don't like emergency medicine as much as you thought, and you want to switch."

Abruptly, her stomach stopped roiling. In fact, it stopped doing much of anything, because now it was on the floor. "I don't see how you're getting that."

"For one thing, you didn't deny it just now. No, don't try now—I'm just pointing out a fact. For another thing, you always want more time with patients, when in EM, you have to be okay without having that. It's a core part of it, and that doesn't make you a bad doctor, but it does make you maybe not suited to this."

Daphne swallowed back her rising bile. "That's not your call to make."

Vibol's tone softened, but only slightly. "I'm not making a call. I'm telling you what I observe. Emergency medicine is nonstop chaos and patients you don't get to know before they're sent somewhere else, and I just don't think you like that." Daphne opened her mouth to retort, but he shook his head. "Did I ever tell you my brother switched specialties?"

Vibol's older brother was a wildly successful neurosurgeon out in Seattle and something of a legend among their group. "Wait, really?"

"He was cardiology for two years, then finally admitted he was miserable and found someone who was willing to swap places in his residency program. Meant he had to take a little longer to finish, but he said it was worth it."

"Good for him, I guess."

Vibol sent her a dirty look. "You see what I'm getting at, right?"

"I do, but you're wrong, okay? I just had a few off days."

"You said weeks."

"Or weeks, whatever."

"Just—think about it, Daph. If you're not happy, you don't have to stay."

"I thought you liked to say that being happy is stupid, you just need to make money."

"Sure, but that's me. You're different."

Henry and Ellie joined them, slightly out of breath but grinning. "What are we talking about?"

Daphne panicked, but for once in his life, Vibol apparently decided to let her off the hook. *Michelle must be really rubbing off on him,* she thought, as he shrugged. "Just Daphne being unusually funny these days," he said, and she sent him a silent thank-you.

"Aww, did our girl make a joke?" Ellie said.

"Hey, I think Daphne's quite funny," Henry protested, and Ellie, Vibol, and Daphne all broke out in laughter.

"That's sweet," Daphne said, patting his hand. "But really, they're right. I'm not."

"It's why we love her," Ellie said.

"We love who?" Michelle asked, sitting down next to Vibol and scooting her chair closer to him.

"Daphne the Unfunny," Vibol explained.

"Oh no, did she do a knock-knock joke again?"

"Hey, that was one time," Daphne said.

"Yeah, one real bad time," Vibol muttered into his drink.

"We should dance, Henry," Daphne announced.

"With pleasure, my lady," he said, and stood up to bow.

Chapter Twenty-Five

Daphne had never been one to laze about in bed in the mornings. That just wasn't her style, not when there were classes to study for or work to be done. But now, with Henry, she wanted to luxuriate in every second, lounge about with him while she could. Outside the sky was bright blue and the sun threw a warm rectangle onto her bed, where she lay on her stomach, the crossword puzzle book open in front of her. She tapped the pen against her lips, thinking.

"Another word for *thwart*. Five letters," she said.

Henry had been resting on his side next to her, trailing his fingertips along her spine, sending pleasant shivers across her skin. He leaned over and moved her hair to the side, placing a tender kiss on the nape of her neck. "Avert?"

Daphne wrote his suggestion down, and whined only a little when he tugged the book out of her hand and placed it on the nightstand. Henry tucked her under his arm, with her head pillowed on his chest. She listened to the cadence of his heart, beating a steady, comforting rhythm. She heard heartbeats all day at work, but it was different through a stethoscope than it was with her ear pressed against his bare skin. "It's getting warmer out," Henry observed, looking at the window.

Daphne didn't want to reply, because she knew what he meant underneath that otherwise bland observation—it was getting warmer because the summer solstice was rapidly bearing down on them.

"What if you stayed?" she asked, the words slipping out without thinking. Henry's fingers stopped trailing idly across her bare shoulder. "I mean, I know you can't, but what would it be like, do you think?"

"You're a dangerous woman, Daphne," he rumbled.

She smiled against his skin. "Your accent gets thicker in bed."

"No, it gets thicker when I'm relaxed," he said, gathering her in his arms and kissing the top of her head. Henry let out a long breath and started speaking. "I think, if I were to stay, I'd like to get a job."

"I'd hope so. Otherwise you'd just be freeloading off me," Daphne teased.

He chuckled. "I was thinking about cooking, actually. Perhaps in a restaurant."

"A chef?"

"Or a chef's assistant—what's the word? Sous chef? I don't think I'm good enough to be the head of a kitchen. Not yet, anyway."

"Don't sell yourself short," she pushed.

"I'm not, I'm just acknowledging I have a long way to go," Henry countered. "And even if I couldn't find work as a chef, I think I'd like to keep cooking. It's—don't laugh, but it's a way for me to show people I care for them, and I never had that before."

Daphne propped her chin on his chest, chewing her lower lip. "I'm sure your mother and sisters know you care for them."

"Aye, but not like this. I provide for them, and I listen to them, but showing it—expressing it, like this—that's not something I ever considered before."

"You're a caretaker. It's part of you."

"It is," he agreed. "And it's a part of you."

She hid her face. "Don't. We're talking about you."

"And I want to talk about you." He curled his finger under her chin and lifted it to meet his gaze. "If I stayed, what would you do differently?"

"I'd leave emergency medicine," Daphne admitted, and her chest loosened from a tightness she hadn't even noticed.

"Then you should when I leave," he said seriously.

"I don't—I know I should, but knowing that and doing it are two different things, Henry."

"Why?"

"Because." Henry waited for her to complete the thought, and when she didn't, he lifted an eyebrow. Daphne sighed. "Because it means shattering my plan, okay? I know it seems small to you, because it's not like I'm talking about leaving medicine, but this has been such a big part of my life plan, and I don't know if I can lose that if I lose you, too."

"But you'd be happier if you switched."

"Maybe. Probably, I don't know. I don't even know if it's possible; I know it happens, but it's hard and a lot of things have to go right for it to work."

"Never thought you'd shy away from a challenge."

"It's not that, it's—fuck, I don't know, Henry, but the past few months have been so disorienting, you know? Meeting you and falling for you and now—" The lump in her throat made it impossible to force the next few words out.

"And now you're losing me," Henry finished. "That's no reason to sentence yourself to unhappiness, my love."

Daphne smiled weakly and stretched her neck to kiss him. "What will you do back there?" she asked.

"Be miserable," he deadpanned. He cupped her cheek in his hand and looked at her thoughtfully. "Go back to my old life. Provide for my mother, find my sisters suitable husbands—or let them find them themselves," he corrected before she could interject. "Run the business, I guess."

"You won't get married?" Daphne asked, hesitant. She wasn't sure how she wanted him to respond.

Henry looked deep into her eyes, his gaze an impossibly bright blue. "Not if I can't have you."

Daphne looked away first. "That's no reason to sentence yourself to unhappiness," she echoed.

"Would you? Marry?"

"I always thought I would, but not in a specific, 'this is what I want' way. More that it just seemed like the next step, and I sort of vaguely assumed it would happen. I just never thought it would be a nineteenth-century gentleman."

"If I stayed, would we?"

"I'd marry you, yes," Daphne said, surprised by both her own certainty and the ease with which she admitted it. "I'd marry you, Henry MacDonald, if you'd have me."

"Of course I would, woman," he said, cuffing his hand around the back of her neck to kiss her.

Daphne smiled even though her heart was splintering into a thousand tiny shreds. "Would we have kids?"

Henry considered her thoughtfully. "In my time, that's not much of a choice, barring unforeseen issues. But if you want them, I'd be happy to have them with you."

She made herself laugh even as tears pricked the corners of her eyes. "What do we do, Henry? You have to go home, and the portal won't open for another seven years."

"Don't wait for me," Henry replied. "It's too long, and life is far too uncertain. Live your life, and find happiness, Daph. Find it, no matter what."

"Only if you promise the same thing," she whispered hoarsely.

Henry didn't answer, just kissed her like it was the last thing he would ever do.

Chapter Twenty-Six

"This smells amazing," Michelle said, walking through the door. She had a bottle of red wine in her left hand, Vibol close on her heels with a bottle of white.

Henry looked up from the stove. "Chicken tikka masala, gyoza, and a salad with goat cheese and cranberries," he explained.

"Tikka masala *and* gyoza?" Vibol asked. "You know those are not from the same regions despite being from the Asian continent, right?"

"Right," Henry said. He turned a burner off and started ladling the tikka masala into a bowl. "But it's my going-away dinner, and these are the two best things I've had while I'm here."

Daphne knew the unspoken words behind his explanation were *I won't be able to have them at home*, which broke her heart. Henry had been so interested in and excited by the way food had evolved since his time, but now that he was going back, he wasn't going to be able to recreate most of it.

"What's with the salad?" Michelle asked. Daphne opened the bottle of wine she'd brought and started pouring, while Michelle ferried the glasses to the table.

"Daphne's favorite," Henry said with a warm smile. "And we have dessert, too."

"Dessert?" Brittany asked interestedly. She toed her shoes off and padded into the kitchen. "What's for dessert?"

"Lava cakes," Ellie said from where she sat at the table, sipping wine. "It's smelled amazing in here all day, been absolute *torture*."

"Then let's eat," Vibol declared. For a short time, everyone busied themselves serving and passing bowls around. There were mountains of fluffy white rice and perfectly stuffed gyoza, and the chicken tikka masala was a glowing golden red against the green of the salad.

"What food will you miss the most?" Ellie asked, chewing.

"That macaroni and cheese that comes out of a box," Henry said sheepishly. "It's the most delicious thing I've ever eaten, even if it's not that much fun to make."

"Processed food really is one of our better inventions," Brittany agreed.

Once they had made their way through dinner—and while Vibol was right, tikka masala and gyoza didn't go together, that didn't make either any less delicious—and Henry had served the molten lava cakes, he stood up expectantly. "At the risk of sounding, as you all are so fond of accusing me, *cheesy*, I would like to say something."

Daphne's throat felt thick and her eyes blurred, but when Henry picked up his glass of wine, she did the same. "I know adopting a man from nearly two centuries ago was not in any of your plans, but I do appreciate the way you all took me in. And not just that, but you took me in and showed me how the world *could* be, even when it felt strange and foreign to me. Even when I resisted, or was just wrong."

"You were wrong a lot, to be fair," Brittany said dryly.

"I was." He chuckled. "But I've learned, and now, when I go back, I know I'll be a better man. And that's thanks to you." He lifted his wine and everyone followed suit, clinking their glasses together.

Daphne met his gaze, devastated by two equally difficult ideas—she loved Henry more than she'd ever loved anyone before, and she was about to lose him.

◆ ◆ ◆

Daphne stood next to Henry, her hand clasped tightly in his, in a semicircle with the rest of her friends. The apartment building to their right was throwing just enough shade to keep them out of the late-afternoon sun, which was currently baking the entire city.

"So we're sure about the exact time of this?" Brittany asked, checking her watch.

"As sure as I can be, and I reran the equation half a dozen times," Ellie said. "And the solstice is at 3:50 p.m. today."

"And we're in the right spot?" Brittany asked.

"It was down there," Henry answered, pointing to an otherwise unremarkable spot on the street a few blocks back. "And Ellie's calculations put the spot here now."

"You're *sure*," Brittany said.

"One doesn't forget the moment they arrived in a new century," Henry said dryly.

"Yeah, but you did get flattened by Daphne right after," Vibol countered.

"He's right—that sort of trauma can cause memories to feel sharp but actually be inaccurate," Michelle added.

"What if I confirm it was right here?" Daphne said with a faint smile.

"That's better than nothing, but still—" Vibol said, looking around. "She did run a dude over with her bike. That's also traumatic."

"He's right, guys," Daphne said firmly. She knew they were being weird because everyone felt a little strange right now. Or rather, *they* felt strange. Daphne had thought she would feel heartbroken, but instead she just felt numb. She was losing Henry within the next few minutes, and all she could do was stand there and hold his hand.

"You've got all the meds, right?" Michelle asked.

They had, after a lot of arguing about "timelines" and "the space-time continuum," agreed to send him with a giant stash of antibiotics, antivirals, and some over-the-counter painkillers, along with a medical textbook. Henry had dutifully written down everything they'd told him about using them, and had sworn he wouldn't dispense medication to anyone except those he knew, to keep from interrupting the next century-plus of medical progress. Henry had wanted to take a photograph back with him, and Vibol had agreed, but Daphne and the rest were worried about what that might do—none of them fully understood time travel, and too much modernity in the 1800s might fuck everything up. Daphne understood why Henry wanted photos, but she thought perhaps it would be easier for him, if he could forget her.

She'd never forget him, obviously. But maybe he could. Maybe he could move on, just like she'd promised him she would, knowing that it was a lie.

"I have everything, just like the last time you asked," Henry said gently. "And thank you all. For this, and for—everything."

"Don't get all sentimental on me now," Vibol chided, but his brown eyes were glistening.

Henry moved first, dropping Daphne's hand to move toward Vibol and draw him into a hug. It was not an awkward, back-patting hug but a true, genuine one. Henry murmured something, and Vibol murmured something back, and when he pulled away, Vibol's eyes went straight to Michelle, answering Daphne's mental question about what Henry had said.

Henry hugged Michelle next, then Brittany, who once again sincerely thanked him for his complete ignorance of contemporary pop icons.

"Two minutes," Ellie announced grimly. Henry hugged Ellie, and nodded slightly as he stepped back, responding to something she said. Daphne made a mental note to ask him about it, then realized—she wouldn't have time.

Their time together was over. She fell into his arms for one last embrace, their kiss tasting of tears, but she wasn't sure if they were hers or his. "I love you, Daphne Griffin," he whispered into her ear. "Don't you ever forget that."

"I love you, too," she replied, fighting to keep her voice steady. "Forever."

"Promise me you'll be happy," he said, holding her hands and stepping back. "Promise me you'll switch."

"Switch?" Ellie said, and Michelle elbowed her with a shushing noise.

"Henry, I—"

"One minute," Brittany said, glancing at Ellie's timer.

"Promise me," he said sternly, and she nodded.

Henry stepped forward to kiss her one last time, and then walked backward toward the spot where they'd first crashed into each other's lives, his hand holding hers as he went. "Goodbye, everyone," he said.

Behind him a sliver of twisting, shimmering light appeared, and Brittany gasped. Henry didn't even look back, just kept his gaze on Daphne. "I love you," Henry said, so quietly only she could hear him.

Then he dropped her hand and stepped backward into the portal.

And then he was gone.

Chapter Twenty-Seven

Silence.

That was the first thing Henry noticed. Wherever he was, it was quiet. No humming motors, no buzz of electricity, no planes roaring overhead.

The second thing he noticed was the darkness. It wasn't black—Edinburgh at night was never fully dark, but it wasn't the bright, artificial white light of the twenty-first century. A gas lamp flickered half a block ahead, and as his eyes adjusted to the lack of light, his ears started to pick up the sounds. Wagon wheels on cobblestone, horseshoes clip-clopping, and harnesses rattling.

I wonder what Daphne would think. The thought flitted across his mind before he had a chance to quash it. Thinking of Daphne and her reaction had become second nature to him in just a few short months, but he needed to start moving past that now, somehow. It knifed through him, the ache sharp.

Henry looked around his surroundings, trying to get his bearings. Edinburgh Castle was limned in moonlight to his left, and the homes around him were spacious but not overly grand, which meant home was straight ahead, perhaps a mile.

Henry turned on his heel and walked in the opposite direction instead. He was worried what he would find at home. Daphne and the others may have shown him what women could be capable of, but that was in a century where their ambition and desires were at least somewhat nurtured; he dreaded returning home to discover that his mother and sisters had somehow already been thrown out of their house, destitute. It wasn't likely, but it wasn't impossible, either. The guilt of having stayed an extra few months in the future gnawed at him now that he was home. Perhaps it had been the wrong choice, as glorious as it had been. Perhaps he had abandoned the people he'd sworn he would always protect. Perhaps he'd been too selfish.

Henry turned right and then veered down a narrow street that felt cramped after the wide, spacious city he'd just left. If his calculations were correct, it would be close to ten at night, which meant George was likely still in his office.

Henry's best friend was what his old—new—future?—friends would call a workaholic. George worked as a solicitor and took his job very seriously, often staying at his small office well into the evening. He had no family to return to in the evenings, as he was fond of pointing out to Henry, so there wasn't any reason not to simply stay and work late. Henry had met him when they were at boarding school (*what a barbaric thing, sending kids away like that,* Daphne had said when he told her how he'd been schooled), both of them reeling from loss. Henry had just lost his father the year before, whereas George had lost his parents to cholera just six months earlier. An only child, he had been sent to live with a wealthy but chilly aunt, who promptly enrolled him in a school just about as far from her home as she could manage.

Neither George nor Henry had ever really felt like they belonged, and they had been fast friends since their first term. But where Henry returned home to run his father's business, George had needed to strike out on his own. He was now a wealthy man in his own right, but aside from Henry and his sisters, George had no family to speak of. The aunt had died when he was twenty, but it wasn't much of a loss, all things considered. She had been a patron, not a parent.

As Henry had suspected, the lamps were still lit in George's office. He considered knocking, but never had done that before, and anyway, he didn't want to risk George thinking he was an impostor or spirit and raising a hue and cry.

Henry shouldered the door open and couldn't help but smile at the familiar sight of George hunched over his desk in the back room, so absorbed in his work he hadn't even looked up. Henry walked to the open door and stood there, waiting.

"If you forgot your watch again, O'Malley, your wife will skin you alive and I'll make sure no judge convicts her," George called, turning a page on whatever he was reading.

"Good thing I'm not O'Malley, then. Nor married, for that matter," Henry replied.

Recognition froze George's muscles in place. He went deathly still and slowly lifted his head, staring at Henry with a cautious hope that hurt for him to see. *It was selfish to have stayed so long.* He'd known that all along, but somehow hoped—he wasn't sure what, but perhaps that his loved ones hadn't missed him all that much. It had been a foolish hope, but he'd hoped it nonetheless.

"Have I gone mad?" George rasped, slowly unfolding his long body from his chair. "Are you real?"

"Very," Henry said, his grin deepening. Leaving Daphne hurt like hell, but he had missed his friend, too. "I'm back."

George nearly knocked over a candle on his desk in his haste to get over to pull Henry into a tight hug. "What—how—where the bloody hell *were* you?" George stammered.

"It's a long story."

"Then tell it," George ordered, holding his hand out to a velvet-covered chair. Henry had been in it countless times, waiting for George to finish his work so they could walk back to Henry's family's mansion together. Sitting in it, with the comfortingly familiar flicker of gaslight and candles, made him curiously homesick. He wasn't sure what he missed, the future or the past. It was all so godforsakenly confusing.

"I went to the future," Henry said bluntly.

George blinked. "Pardon?"

"Where I was, when I was gone. I went to the future. Time-traveled, as it were. But I'm back now."

"You cannot be serious."

"Alas, my friend, I am."

George stood, walked to the sideboard behind his desk, and poured a healthy glass of whisky. He downed it in one gulp, then poured another measure, before pouring another glass for Henry. "You're going to have to start from the beginning."

So he did. George listened without questioning him. Henry found himself telling the story as though Daphne were just one of the kind people who took him in, not the woman he'd fallen in love with, but he didn't have time or, as Brittany was fond of putting it, the "executive function" to figure out why he was doing so.

"Women doctors are common?" George asked disbelievingly when Henry was done.

"Indeed," Henry confirmed. "And they get quite cross if you are surprised by that fact."

"I'll have to remember that if I ever go to the future," George said dryly. "Are they . . . pretty?"

Daphne's face flashed before him, but Henry blinked it away. "Some are."

"And you're quite sure you time-traveled? You weren't locked in a madhouse and have only just escaped?"

Henry reached into his knapsack and drew out one of the photographs he had promised Daphne he wouldn't bring back to the past. Not the one he knew he couldn't survive without but the other one, the one of them in the formal outfits at the hospital gala. Vibol with his arm around Michelle's waist, Brittany and Ellie in the middle, and Henry and Daphne on the other end of the line, all of them beaming at the photographer.

George studied it, his brow furrowed. It wasn't that he had never seen a photograph before, but rather the way it was printed. "It's in color?" he asked after several long seconds. "Not colored after the fact, but—" He flipped it over, judging the weight of the paper and running his fingertips along the back. "This was printed this way. And these clothes—what trick is this?"

"It's no trick. This is how photographs are, in the future." Henry paused, considering trying to explain that most of them had all their photographs on little rectangles they carried in their pockets and called "phones" even though mostly they just sent tiny, short missives back and forth, rather than talking, and decided against it.

He could explain that to George later. He had all the time in the world now.

George had stopped looking at the photograph and now studied him just as intensely. "Who did you leave?"

"Those people. They became very good friends," Henry replied over the lump in his throat. He'd never lied to George before and wasn't sure why he was doing so now, but admitting his feelings for Daphne might shatter whatever reserve he was clinging to, and he didn't want to break down. Not here, not now.

It didn't look as though George believed him, but he nodded nonetheless. He checked his pocket watch. "Your mother and sisters have likely gone to bed, but I'm sure they'd want to be woken. I assume you haven't gone there yet?"

"Not yet," Henry admitted. "I didn't want—I needed to be sure, I guess. That I really was back. And I returned closer to you," he lied. Two lies in barely two minutes—perhaps George's friend hadn't really returned from the future.

"We should go, then. Maggie will have my head if she finds out I knew you were alive and kept you from her. And Henry?"

"Yes?"

"I'm glad you're home."

Henry had to remind himself that *home* no longer meant Daphne, but he nodded.

Chapter Twenty-Eight

Henry's insides felt like a bucket of eels, twisting and turning as he walked toward the home his father had bought for them the year before his death. It had been brand new then, but nigh twenty years on, it was more weathered, the wisteria climbing the front heavy and gnarled at the base. Henry considered letting himself in, but George pointed out that was a sure way to get a coal shovel to the face courtesy of Shepard. The butler had been a boxer at the warehouses down near the docks before entering the family's service, and even with his bum shoulder, Henry didn't fancy being on the receiving end of his attack.

George noticed his hesitation but made no comment, just rang the bell. The windows were dark, the house quiet, but after several seemingly endless minutes, Henry saw the dim light of Shepard's lamp floating across the front hall. "Who is—Mr. Campbell, whatever is wrong?" Shepard asked, his familiar broad frame filling the door. He didn't even glance at Henry.

"Found something that might belong to you," George said, and stepped aside. That slight movement allowed the moonlight to fall straight onto Henry, and Shepard nearly dropped his lamp in shock.

"Mr. MacDonald? Is that truly you? We thought you'd drowned," Shepard said in a voice very unlike his usual stern baritone.

"It's me, Shepard," Henry said. "Alive and well."

"Truly?"

"Truly. Is it—may I come in?"

Training finally overcame Shepard's shock, and he stepped aside hastily. "Of course, of course. What would you like to eat? Wherever you came from, you must be hungry. I'll wake Cook, and then—"

"I'd like to see my mother first," Henry said gently.

"Oh, of course, sir, I'm so sorry, I wasn't thinking. Lyd—Mrs. MacDonald will of course want to see you right away. I'll send for a maid and tell her to wake your mother."

Henry noticed Shepard's unusual slip of the tongue but filed it away to ask about later, when everyone was a little less flustered. "My sisters too, if you please. But—don't tell them why, just tell them not to be worried."

"Of course, sir, right away, sir," Shepard said, and hurried away, his dressing gown flapping in a slightly undignified manner.

George grabbed a candle on a nearby table and lit it. Henry considered how short a time it had been since he'd left, but how accustomed he'd become to modern conveniences—in the twenty-first century, that light would have been provided by flipping a switch, and while it was a colder, more impersonal light, it was far simpler.

They let themselves into the front parlor, where the fire was banked for the evening. Henry lit the gas lamps on the wall, which had felt like the height of luxury when he had them installed and now felt oddly primitive. It would take some time for him to adjust to the past—present?—that much was clear. George busied himself with the fire, which was soon roaring cheerfully. This far north it was still chilly of an evening, and Henry appreciated the warmth chasing away the damp chill of a June night.

"What's it like, then? The future?" George asked.

"It's—different," Henry started. "They have so much, especially electricity. Everything's powered by it, and they have carriages that drive themselves. No horses, just an engine, and a wheel that they use to direct it."

George furrowed his brow. "Sounds fantastical."

Once again, Daphne's face flashed before his eyes, and a stab of pain went through his chest. "It is," he replied with some difficulty.

"What's wrong—" George started, but then the door swung open and Lydia MacDonald strode in.

"George, I know you're one of the family, but why on earth are you here at this ungodly—" Lydia stopped, and her jaw dropped as her gaze finally fixed on her oldest child. "No. No. It can't be," she whispered in an agonized voice. "We—we lost you."

"You didn't, Ma," Henry said, using a term for her he'd dropped sometime around his father's death. "I'm here. I'm alive."

"Oh, Henry," Lydia said, and burst into uncharacteristic tears. The last time Henry had seen his mother weep was when he was seventeen, when his uncle had gotten the business deep in debt. But those had been tears of frustration, not gladness, and Henry wrapped his mother in his arms, reminding himself that this was why he'd returned. Staying with Daphne would have meant letting his family believe him dead, which would have been unimaginably cruel.

He could give her up, for this. He had, and it was the right thing to do. "Mama, Gwendolyn said we have a visitor, but whoever would call at this time of night?" Maggie asked as she walked in, pausing mid-stride. "Henry?" she asked in a quiet voice.

Anne was close on her heels, and she was the first to come to her senses. "Henry!" she squealed, and ran into his arms, suddenly a precocious eleven-year-old again and not a young woman of nineteen. "I knew you weren't dead, I knew it," Anne crowed. "Didn't I tell you, Mama?"

Lydia wiped her cheeks and sniffled noisily. "You'll need to forgive me for not believing you, but it just didn't seem possible."

"Where *were* you?" Maggie demanded. "It doesn't seem like you to just run away, so—kidnapped? By pirates?"

"That was what I said." Anne pouted.

"No, you said *Vikings*, which is ridiculous because there haven't been Vikings in centuries."

"Girls, girls," Lydia tried ineffectively.

"No, I said there might be some sort of veil through time, and maybe a Viking slipped through. That's different."

"If possible, it's even more ridiculous when Henry was probably just held for ransom by highwaymen." Maggie sniffed. "Weren't you, Henry?"

"Wouldn't the ransom demand have been sent here?" George interjected.

"Not if he escaped," Maggie replied.

"I was not kidnapped by Vikings, pirates, or highwaymen," Henry said before George set off a new round of bickering between his sisters. "But Anne was more accurate than you'd think."

Lydia sat down, back ramrod straight, on the settee. "Then you should explain. Shall I ring for some tea?"

But Shepard walked in then with a tray of tea and bannocks, as always anticipating his mother's desires before she even expressed them. "Thank you, Shep," she said affectionately.

"Aren't you going to give your brother a hug?" George needled Maggie.

Ever the grump, Maggie glared at him and marched over to give Henry a surprisingly gentle hug. "Welcome back, brother," she murmured, and he squeezed her tight before letting go.

Lydia poured them all tea and everyone settled down, the only sounds the rustle of the ladies' wrappers and the soft clink of teacups to saucers. "So, wherever you have been these past five months, it must have been somewhere very far away, for you to not have been able to send word."

Henry met his mother's shrewd gaze and nodded. "It was. I was in America."

"America has the post, if I recall correctly," Maggie pointed out.

"I was in America, but not in 1885. I was in the future. The twenty-first century, to be exact."

Anne's eyes widened as big as dinner plates. "A time veil?"

"We called it a portal, but in brief, yes."

"We?" Maggie asked. "Who's *we*?"

"I made some friends there," Henry said, feeling worse each time he denied Daphne her rightful place in his heart. "They took me in, kept me safe."

Maggie and Lydia exchanged a look. "How do you know that's, er, where you went?" Maggie asked.

"I haven't gone mad, I promise."

"He's got proof," George said. "I believe him."

Maggie looked skeptical, but Lydia's shoulders eased slightly. "I'll show you when I'm done," Henry said. "But I need to explain first."

"I want to know about the time veil. What was it like? Is it still open? Can I go?" Anne asked.

Henry smothered a grin at her eagerness. More than any of them, Anne would be well suited to the future. "It's like stepping into an abyss—you fall, but only for a moment, and then you're somewhere else. Some-when else, actually."

"Why did you choose to go through it?" Maggie asked.

"I didn't. I thought it was smoke or haze, not a rip in time."

"And then?" Anne asked.

"I thought I'd fallen and hit my head. I did fall, actually—a woman on a bicycle rode straight into me and knocked me over."

A woman felt like a paltry way to refer to the only woman he'd love for the rest of his life, but he had already committed to the omission.

"A woman? On a bicycle?" Anne asked excitedly.

"A woman doctor," Henry said, and Anne sat up straight.

"A doctor? She was admitted to a medical school as a student, not just an observer?"

"A doctor in every sense of the word," Henry said, unable to keep the pride out of his voice. "In the future, a lot of women are. There's a lot of things like that: most women work; they don't stay home. Not just poor women, but wealthy women, too."

Lydia raised her eyebrows. "They must have a lot of servants to run their houses."

"They don't, but they have a lot of technology that makes up for it. A machine that washes clothes, for instance. And another one that dries them."

"A machine to dry clothes? Who ever heard of such a ridiculous thing," Lydia replied. "Is there no sun or wind in the future?"

"It goes much faster," Henry argued. "Everything there is faster, really. It's all instantaneous, or so close to being so that it makes no matter."

"Where did you stay?" asked Maggie, always the taskmaster.

"With—the friends I made. They lived in a sort of tenement building, and for a while I was in an empty flat, and then when the occupant returned, I stayed with some of them."

"That must have been ghastly, sharing a tenement," Anne said, making a face.

"It's actually quite nice. Nothing like the ones you're thinking of. The future is so different from what we think it will be, as a matter of fact."

From there his family had fewer questions, or perhaps so many more they couldn't decide how to articulate them. Like with George, Henry made his decision to stay longer a little fuzzy; rather than deciding he couldn't say goodbye to a woman, which felt unimaginably selfish after seeing how overjoyed his family was to have him back, he made it sound like there'd been a miscalculation on the time, leading to him missing the window to return. There were a few times he couldn't avoid mentioning Daphne entirely, and both times Anne's eyes narrowed slightly, but she stayed silent.

"And then I went to George's office first, as I was sure he'd still be there, before we came straight here," Henry finished.

Lydia's cup was empty and she stood, pulling him up for another hug. "Welcome home," she whispered. "I never dared hope. When you didn't return home that day, I thought you'd slipped into the Firth and drowned. You're a fair swimmer, but not a strong one, and the waves were big that day."

"I'm sorry," he murmured into his mother's grey hair. "I would have come back that day, if I could." That, at least, wasn't a lie.

Lydia stepped back and wiped one more tear from her cheek. "I think this calls for a celebration. Cook shouldn't be woken at this time of night, but Shep—Shepard can find something more hearty than this in the kitchen for us."

"I'll cook," Henry offered without thinking.

The reaction was immediate. He might as well have fired a cannon into the parlor. Maggie laughed, George scoffed, and his mother huffed, "Well, I never." Only Anne seemed less than mortally offended by his suggestion. Even though he'd known that it wasn't common in his time for men—especially men of his status—to cook, he hadn't considered how alien it would seem to his loved ones.

"You cook?" Lydia sputtered.

"Do men in the future really do that?" Anne asked.

Henry shrugged. "Some do, some don't, just as some women in the future do, and some don't."

"What on earth has happened to society there?" Maggie demanded.

"It sounds ghastly," George said. "When you said no servants, I assumed there would at least be a cook."

"You won't have to do that anymore, darling," Lydia said. "Shepard can manage to find a few more things for us to eat."

The reality set in for Henry all at once. A wealthy man doing his own cooking just wasn't done in the nineteenth century unless he wanted to be called "eccentric." Henry's family were still strivers, despite their money, and he would need to follow the rules of society as they existed once again.

He would go back to the import business too, with the endless columns of numbers and lists and bills of lading. Regret coupled with grief for the life he'd left behind rose up inside him, and he wondered if this was what it would always be like now, never feeling at home in his time, always feeling out of place. He'd spent so long in the twenty-first century yearning for the past, and now that he was back, he was yearning for the future.

Chapter Twenty-Nine

"What's in your knapsack?" Anne asked around a mouthful of cold roast chicken, nodding toward the pack he'd left against the wall. George and Maggie were discussing a ship that had been delayed by a storm, while Lydia spoke softly to Shepard in the corner.

The gang had had several conversations about the ethics of sending him back with modern medicine, as *what about paradoxes* was something most of them seemed gravely concerned with, despite not being able to sufficiently explain the issue to him. However, in the end they'd packed him up with half a dozen different medicines and an old pharmacological textbook, with the caveat that he had to immediately promise to write a will wherein that book would be burned upon his death, to lessen the chance of "breaking the space-time continuum."

"Medicines, mostly," he said, and Anne's eyes lit up.

"What sort? Tonics? Something for pain?"

"A few for pain, but the rest are for infections. There's a book that explains how to use them, but we have to be careful, as these haven't been invented or discovered yet."

Anne furrowed her brow. "Why does that matter?"

Henry sighed. "No one would really explain, but I guess things are supposed to happen in a specific order, and they're worried that if something happens too early, it could keep other important things from happening."

But Anne was eyeing his backpack and clearly not really listening. "Can I see them? You said some are for infections, and I've been reading some research coming out of Germany about infections caused by tiny living organisms. Does this kill those organisms?"

"That's roughly what happens, yes. There's a book that explains how it works as well."

Anne nearly shoved him over in her haste to get to the bag. "Really and truly? Can I read it? I promise, I won't tell a soul."

Henry laughed, his sister's brightness reminding him that coming back had been the honorable thing to do. "You may. I won't be able to explain much, but they taught me the basics."

"And it's common for women to be doctors? That wasn't just you saying so?"

"I personally knew four women doctors, all of them brilliant. And it wasn't seen as at all unusual."

Anne sighed wistfully. "I wish I could travel to the future."

"The portal won't open for another seven years. But I wish you could; you'd love it there. It's fun, Annie. So much fun."

Anne blinked. "Who are you, and what have you done with my *women should learn to be happy with what they have, lest they risk being miserable* brother?"

"He went to the future and learned he'd been a downright ass to you." *And he was unhappy with his lot in life and terrified you'd end up the same way.*

"Did the future also make you forget your manners?" Anne said, looking a little surprised at his crude language.

Henry chuckled ruefully. "It did a little, yes."

"Well then. Thinking you might be dead was awful, but if you're back and less of a miserable prat, I guess you falling through a time veil isn't so bad."

"I'm sorry I didn't come home sooner," he said.

"Nonsense, you came as soon as you could manage," Anne said, digging through his bag to find the textbook from Vibol. "What's this?" she added, picking up a small, stiff rectangle that had fluttered to the floor.

It was a photo of him and Daphne on the dance floor at the gala, lost in each other. Ellie had printed it for him, and he'd smuggled it back in between the pages of the book, unwilling to leave all proof of his feelings for Daphne in the future.

"It's a photograph," he said around a suddenly tight throat.

Anne studied it closely. "Ahhh," she said quietly. "I see."

"She's one of the doctors I was telling you about," Henry said, attempting to sound as though he were discussing Brittany or Ellie and not the love of his life.

"Mm-hmm," Anne said. "She's pretty."

She's beautiful. "She is. Was. Will be? I haven't quite figured out how to talk about the future, given that it's also my past."

"Nice try, big brother. I won't be so easily distracted. You really left her behind? For us?"

"I had to, Annie. I couldn't let you all believe I'd deserted you."

"We never thought that. We grieved, of course. Mama didn't get out of bed for a week once we realized you wouldn't be coming home, and Maggie threw herself into running the business but barely slept. But we never thought you'd simply abandoned us."

"And what did you do?"

Anne smiled sadly. "I went into your room every day to read a book."

Guilt washed over him. He shouldn't have stayed just to break his own heart. He should have come home right away, saved them all the pain, himself included. "I'm so sorry," he whispered.

"I know," Anne said. "But you're back, and that's what matters."

Across the room, Maggie yawned behind her hand and George stood up. "We should get some sleep and resume our festivities in the morning," he suggested.

"I'll have to go check out the docks, see what's happening," Henry pointed out.

"I can take you," Maggie suggested. "I want your opinion on a few things."

"How about supper, then?" George suggested.

"I'll have Cook draw up a menu. Would you want to invite anyone else, ma'am?" Shepard asked Lydia.

"No one else yet. I'll put out that he's back from his trip to America, but that we want to wait a few days before throwing an official soiree."

"My trip?"

"In case you did come back," Maggie said with a shrug. "We knew you weren't, or I guess we thought we knew you weren't, but since we didn't know for sure—"

"Mama didn't want Uncle Stephen trying to run the business again," Anne interjected.

"Hush," Lydia said.

"Your bedroom is still made up, Mr. MacDonald," Shepard said. "We let Higgins go after—ah, your disappearance, but I could wake a footman."

Higgins was Henry's valet, having been hired just a few weeks before he traveled. "No need, let them sleep." He'd been dressing himself for months, and it would take some time to get used to having servants do that for him. "Did Higgins find a new position?"

"I could ask around, but I believe so, sir. We did give him an excellent character reference, of course."

"Of course. But for tonight, I'll see to myself, and we can handle that tomorrow." The habits of being a rich man in the 1880s were slowly coming back to him, but they felt like an ill-fitting pair of boots, too stiff in places and too loose in others.

"Just so, sir. Let me get you a candle, and then I'll see Mr. Campbell out."

Lydia came over to give him another tight hug, and Maggie did the same. Anne was absorbed in the medical text, brushing her chin with the end of her braid in an achingly familiar way. "Annie, dearest. We're off to bed," Lydia said gently.

"Can't I—"

"Tomorrow. Whatever that book is, it will still be here tomorrow."

Anne sighed and reluctantly closed it, but she didn't leave it on her chair. Henry knew that if he knocked on her door in an hour, she'd still be awake, curled next to her fire, reading voraciously. "Good night, little sister," he said, and kissed the top of her head.

"Good night, big brother," she echoed with a sweetly innocent smile. Oh yes, she was definitely staying awake the rest of the night.

Henry bade George goodbye and followed his family upstairs. His bedroom was neat, having been kept in good order by the maids, but it still felt foreign. *This will pass,* he reminded himself. *Just as the future felt odd for weeks, this too will seem strange until I'm reaccustomed to it.*

But everything felt wrong. His nightshirt was too scratchy, the sheets cold. The mattress was soft but lumpy, nothing like the glorious clouds they slept on in the future. Even having a fire going in the grate was odd, the noise abruptly unfamiliar. A log cracked and hissed and Henry turned over, wishing above all else for Daphne's warmth beside him.

The past, as it turned out, was a lonely beast.

◆ ◆ ◆

The air near the docks felt familiar, although it did little to lift his spirits. Henry had awoken confused, only to remember that yesterday—yesterday, but also nearly one hundred and fifty years in the future—he had said goodbye to Daphne. Now he was home, where he belonged, and had to go back to his responsibilities. His sojourn to the future had been a lark, an interlude in his life, but it was done and best to put it behind him now.

Maggie, on the other hand, had a spring in her step Henry had never seen before. "Miss MacDonald!" called a dockworker, standing near a stack of barrels. "The captain of the *Fine Lady* said he saw the *Robert Burns* just a day or so ago, going slow but steady. She'll need some repairs but should make it safely."

"Oh good, I'm glad she's intact," Maggie said, drawing to a stop. Henry had never seen his sister interact with anyone outside their social station, aside from servants, and he was struck by her ease almost as much as the practical work boots she had on under her petticoats. "With the storm last week, I feared the worst."

"Aye, I know. But like I told ye, it's nothing she hasn't handled before. Captain Hanson is one of the best."

"Thank you, Peter," Maggie said, and they kept on walking, Peter apparently not having recognized Henry. In fact, he'd barely spared Henry a glance at all, and to be fair, Henry didn't recognize Peter—perhaps he was someone who had unloaded for them in the past, but he only knew the foremen at the docks, not every individual worker. At the time he'd felt like a fair-minded businessman, but he could see Daphne pursing her lips and shaking her head at him.

As he and Maggie walked to the warehouse, that scene repeated itself several times, each man eager to share with her a bit of news. Two more men told them the *Robert Burns* was on its way, while another stopped her to let her know the shipment of timber from yesterday had some flaws, and he was worried she was being taken advantage of by their Norwegian supplier. "I'm well aware of the flaws, John, but I didn't buy that timber for shipwrights. It's bound for a paper mill, and structural flaws don't matter much when it comes to paper." Rather than being chagrined at being gently chastised, John had nodded respectfully and returned to his work.

"A paper mill? We don't have any paper mill clients," Henry observed.

"We didn't. We do now," Maggie said. She unlocked the door to the office that Henry had come to dread, but it looked different. Brighter, somehow. "I cleaned the windows," Maggie explained with a toss of her dark head. "You let it get frightfully dingy in here. You'll ruin your eyesight if you let it get like that again, so mind that you don't."

Henry nodded, taking it in. Most was as he'd left it, but with Maggie's mark left everywhere—the neat stack of papers on one table, and a large map now pinned to the wall behind him, tiny colored tacks scattered across the ocean. "I keep track of the ships, based on expected travel times and any weather events. There was a storm four days ago, and even despite that, the *Robert Burns* should have made it to berth by yesterday evening, so there likely is some sort of damage, even if *Fine Lady*'s crew says she looked whole." She moved one red tack a few inches to the left, bringing it closer to Edinburgh.

"And the paper mill?"

Maggie ran her tongue over her teeth, thinking. "I've made some changes to how you ran things."

"I can see that. I'm not upset, Mags. This looks brilliant already. I just want to know what I'm taking over."

Annoyance flickered across Maggie's face. "You simply took over what Father had left, which was obviously successful, but . . ."

"But?" he prompted.

"But it was stagnating, Henry. Mama did a good job of keeping Uncle Stephen from racking up too much debt before you took over, and you did a fine job at keeping it going. But a business can't just do what was always done, and anyway, I don't believe we'll have much to do with shipbuilding for much longer, anyway. Steamships are clearly going to take over, and if we want to keep up our relationships with timber companies in Scandinavia, we needed to figure out where to send it."

"Thus, paper," Henry said, idly flipping through an account book. The hand in it was familiar, but it wasn't Maggie's.

"Thus, paper," Maggie agreed. "Mama's been helping, too. She can do a lot of sums in her head, said it was all that menu planning us ladies have to do, but between you and me, I think she just likes arithmetic."

"This—" Henry thumbed through the book, trying to make sense of the figures. "This can't be right. In only five months?"

Maggie tried to hide the swell of pride, but Henry could see right through her. "By the end of next month, we'll have added almost a third to our usual import tallies."

Henry's eyebrows hit his hairline and he whistled softly. He had known, of course, that his family was capable of surviving without him, but he hadn't expected them to *excel* in his absence. "Who does the firm belong to now?" Women could own some property, but if either sister married, it would become her husband's instead.

"You, still. Mama was worried about someone trying to take it from us, so we put about that you were on a trip to America, which apparently wasn't a lie. We just had some details wrong. But that way, if Anne or I were to marry, it would stay with Mama."

Something cold settled in his gut. They were fine without him, which was comforting but also devastating, because he had come *back* to help them. Maybe if he'd come back the first time, he could have realized this and then—no, he couldn't think that way. He couldn't contemplate a world where he returned to Daphne for good, because that wasn't possible anymore. In seven years' time, she would have moved on. He wanted her to; she deserved happiness. But maybe it didn't have to be this way, and that knowledge threatened to crack his splintering heart in two.

"Henry? Are you all right?"

"Fine, Mags. Just impressed," he said, and Maggie, always a little less perceptive than Anne, merely nodded with her head a little higher.

Chapter Thirty

It was a typical Scottish fall day—warm but not hot, with the sky an uncertain mix of sun and clouds, as if the sky woke up that day and couldn't decide which way to be. A grey cloud would scud in front of the sun and everything would cool slightly, but then the sun would slide out the other side of the cloud and Henry would feel just a tad too warm.

Arthur's Seat provided a stunning view of Edinburgh itself, and on a Sunday morning, despite his mother's scandalized protesting, Henry felt far closer to God here than he ever had in church. Or perhaps he had simply grown accustomed to the twenty-first-century habit of sleeping in on Sundays rather than going to church, and this was his compromise. For the nearly three months he'd been back, he had spent every Sunday up there, rather than in the pews with his mother and sisters. There were only a few others scattered around the top of the Seat, everyone else more afraid for their mortal souls, apparently. Church bells clamored distantly, and Henry stayed where he was, sitting on a lone boulder, watching the shadows of clouds chase each other across the city.

He was spending more and more time like this, lately. Maggie wasn't just assisting him with MacDonald's Imports, as she kept insisting; she was running it, with Lydia serving as the second-in-command. Henry's name needed to be on documents to keep it safe, but otherwise he was entirely superfluous. He had thought the relief of being back with his family would help with the gut-wrenching ache he felt every time he thought of Daphne, but instead, he just felt worse. His family loved him, but they didn't need him, not the way he had assumed. And he loved them, but he didn't need them—he needed Daphne.

Even worse, he wanted her, and he couldn't stop thinking about his mistakes. Maybe he should have told her how he felt earlier, long before he thought even she suspected her own feelings for him, but it had felt too soon, amid the chaos of him learning an entirely new way of life. But maybe if he'd done so, he could have returned to the nineteenth century, set his affairs in order, and then returned to the twenty-first. Then again, perhaps that wasn't the ironclad plan it appeared, as just a few weeks after his arrival in the twenty-first century, Maggie and Lydia might not have yet figured out their strengths for running the business.

It was just all so damned complicated, and Henry couldn't help but feel like no matter what he had done, it would have been the wrong thing.

Footsteps approached behind him and stopped. "It isn't like you to brood like this," George said.

"I'm not brooding."

"You are," George argued. "It's understandable, though. I'd brood too if I left the love of my life behind in a different century."

"I didn't—"

"Tell me? No, you didn't, but you didn't have to tell me about Sophia, either. I still knew, didn't I?"

George was the only one privy to that particular heartbreak of his, and had in fact figured out Henry's true feelings for Sophia before he'd even admitted them to himself. "How did you know?"

George flicked the tails of his coat behind him to sit next to Henry on the rock. "You've told us a lot about the people you met in the future, but Daphne remains an enigma, which tells me either you didn't know her well—unlikely, given that she ran you down, and she looks like a Renaissance painting of Venus."

"And I have a particular affinity for Venus?" Henry asked wryly.

"You have a particular affinity for *pretty women*, and calling Daphne merely pretty feels like an insult."

That much, at least, was accurate. "It doesn't matter. I can't go back there."

"Why did you come back here, then? If you loved her?"

"My family needed me. Or I thought they did. But that was just me being an arrogant ass, as Daphne liked to call me before—well, before. They didn't need me to save them. Maggie and Mother have the business well in hand, better than I ever did, and I'm left wondering what I'll do with myself now."

"Be a man of leisure? Plenty of men don't work. You and I are some of the only boys we went to school with who don't just live off their estates."

"I don't want that, though. Don't laugh, but in the future, there are a lot of jobs open to everyone, not just women or the poor. I started cooking, and I found I liked it."

"There are chefs here, you know."

"I know. But—" Henry sighed. "It's not the same."

"Without her," George finished.

"Precisely."

"I won't say you made the wrong choice coming back, because I mourned you, brother. It was unspeakably awful, thinking I'd never see you again. But if I never saw you again but knew you were doing the thing you loved with someone you loved, well, I wouldn't like it, but I could make my peace with it."

"I can't go back, George. Not for another seven years, and I made her promise to move on and not wait for me. I wouldn't want her to, even if I thought I could go back in seven years."

"What if you went sooner?"

"There isn't an opening for seven years," Henry said, irritated that George wasn't grasping the central problem.

"Not from Edinburgh to Minneapolis, no, but what if there was one that went elsewhere in America? You said people in the future have faster ways to travel than we do, so what if we just got you to the right time and continent?"

"We?" Henry asked, not daring to hope that the rest of what George had suggested was possible.

"Anne came to my office yesterday with a theory. And she found an equation on a loose piece of paper in that medical textbook."

Ellie's equation. He hadn't thought much about it, since it was only to get him back, but if anyone could figure out a theory to reverse it, it was Anne.

Henry cracked a smile, his first genuine one in weeks. "Of course she did."

"She needs more information from you, what you remember from what you learned, but once she knows how the time veil works, she thinks there's a way to get you back to the right time, if not the exact right place."

"What we need, then, is a Woo-Woo Girl."

"A what now?"

"Ellie called herself that," Henry said, grinning at the memory. "Someone who knows a lot about astrology, cares about the signs, phases of the moon—that sort of thing."

George nodded thoughtfully. "I think I know just the woman."

Chapter Thirty-One

Henry looked at the hand-drawn map in his lap as the countryside smeared by. George's former paramour lived in London, but she had, as he'd claimed, known a lot about constellations and moon phases and "all that woo-woo shit" that everyone liked to tease Ellie about.

"How did I not know about Maria?" Henry asked George. Anne sat across from them, frowning down at a piece of paper.

"You're easy to read and shockingly terrible at noticing things."

Henry grinned. "That makes me sound like an awful friend."

"No, just a very oblivious one. But do you think what Maria said sounds right?"

"I do, yes. The book she had was an earlier version of the one I found. The map in it isn't as detailed as the one I saw in the future, but the title and theory are the same."

"Oh, this is impossible," Anne groaned. She had been immersed in calculations for the better part of an hour, determined to crack it for him. "This makes no *sense*."

George grinned at her. "Never thought I'd see the day where Annie MacDonald gives up."

"I am not *giving up*; I am declaring this an utterly impossible tangle of numbers that only a mathematical genius could decipher."

"I thought you were a genius," Henry teased. "I believe you used to tell me so daily."

Anne fixed them both with an irritated look. "I *am* a genius, but not this particular type of genius. I am a scholar of anatomy and medicine, not numbers and symbols. Those I'm merely brilliant at."

Henry snorted, and wished for the hundredth time she could meet Daphne and her friends.

George, however, was looking thoughtful. "Who could do it, then? Maggie?"

Anne shook her head. "Mags is good at business, but it's Mama who has handled all the numbers. Besides, Maggie would never consent to help get Henry back to the future; she doesn't want him to leave again."

"And you do?" Henry asked mildly.

"Of course. How else will I get uninterrupted use of your books?" Anne replied mischievously, but then she sobered. "George is right, though. We need someone else, and the only one who could do it is Mama."

The three of them shared a look. None of them much fancied approaching Lydia with this, but Anne was right—she was their best shot.

"Then we ask her," Henry said.

"Good," Anne said, handing her stack of calculations over. "But you have to tell Mama you want to leave again alone, because I don't want to be there when you do."

◆ ◆ ◆

Henry knocked on the door to what had been Father's study and waited for Lydia to bid him to enter. She had a ledger open on the desk, a set of spectacles perched on the tip of her nose. It was odd, seeing her in the place Henry had seen as his father's, but it fit, somehow.

"You're back," she announced, somewhat unnecessarily. "I assume it was a productive trip? Was Anne satisfied, or will she continue to wear the same three drab dresses I bought her two seasons ago?"

They hadn't told her the real reason they were going to London, using Anne's need to go shopping for the latest fashions—something she had never once expressed interest in—as their excuse. It was a flimsy pretense, and one he should have realized his mother would see through immediately.

Henry sank into the chair across the desk, chagrined. "It was, but Anne did come home empty-handed."

"Ah. What did you discover, then?"

"A way back through the time veil. Or a possible way back. We hope."

"You hope?"

"Anne started on the calculations, but she couldn't get them to work."

Lydia pursed her lips, sighed, and held out her hand. "Let's see it, then."

Henry hesitated. "If I leave, I am likely not coming back."

"I know." Lydia kept her hand extended, a stern look on her face. "If I could go back in time to see your father, just once more—I would do it. In a heartbeat. So stop stalling and let me see what your sister came up with." Her voice shook ever so slightly as she spoke, at odds with her matter-of-fact tone.

Henry pulled out the book and map with Anne's work scribbled on them and handed them over. He explained the rough outlines of how it worked, but before he could finish, Lydia was nodding to herself, crossing out a few notations, and scribbling down more numbers.

She consulted the map, made one more correction to Anne's calculations, and then nodded once more, satisfied. "There."

"Are you—"

"Of course I'm sure." She handed the map back to him, with an X over a graveyard in a map of Manchester. "It opens outside Manchester three days from now, and will take you to—" She broke off and consulted the book, flipping pages back and forth. "Florida. Isn't that place beastly hot?"

"It is," Henry confirmed, his brain struggling to keep up. "And it's a long way from Minneapolis, but travel is much faster there."

"Then our only real problem is the timing."

"The timing?"

Lydia nodded crisply. "The spacing of the veils—if the calculations are correct, you'll be arriving a year later than you were last there."

That sank in, a cold cube of ice in his stomach. *Only a year—she couldn't have moved on in a year, could she?*

Lydia must have noticed his fear. "What's wrong?"

Henry made himself shrug. "There's many things that could go wrong in a year, that's all."

"You're afraid she'll have moved on." She took off her spectacles, her expression unfamiliarly gentle. "If she loves you, a year won't have been long enough. Believe me on that. Finding love like that again doesn't come easy."

Henry knew Lydia was speaking from experience, but broaching that subject was beyond him at the moment. He swallowed hard, tracing a line with a series of numbers on it from Chicago to Paris. "And if she has?"

"Then in two years, you come back through the veil to Paris. Twenty-four months exactly after your arrival."

It would be a cold two years, living in the future without Daphne, but he couldn't imagine having a chance to see her again and not taking it. "Then that's my plan." He looked up, meeting her direct gaze. "Thank you," he said softly.

Her eyes glistened, and her response came out in a whisper. "Of course."

◆ ◆ ◆

"There are sandwiches in your bag, along with some bannocks," Lydia said, as usual hiding her emotions under business. "Shep can—"

"Shepard doesn't need to do anything else," Henry said soothingly. "It's barely half a day's journey to Manchester."

"Half a day to Manchester, and then across the ocean over a hundred-some years into the future," she corrected.

Henry could have argued, but instead he turned to Maggie, who was waiting impatiently to say goodbye. He opened his mouth, but as usual, his sister beat him to it. "Don't you dare tell me anything about running the business as your final thoughts to me. I don't need any help."

"I was going to say as much." He grinned. "I was never well suited to it, but you—you're brilliant at it, and I'd never dream of pretending I knew better."

"Good," Maggie huffed, but she pulled him into a hug. "I hate that you're leaving, but I do love you, you know."

"I know," he agreed.

Anne's turn was next, although Henry had been up most of the night before, walking her through what the gang had taught him about using the medicines they'd sent and warning about the "space-time paradox" it might cause if word of them or the textbook were to get out. "I have something for you," he said.

Anne looked at his hands eagerly. "Where? What is it?"

"It's not so much a gift as it is an opportunity. I spoke to the medical college, and they have agreed to accept you for the Michaelmas term."

"But that's—"

"Starting in one week, yes. So you had better get prepared. I set the money aside in a trust, but you should be warned: Some of the professors do not want women there, or they charge more for teaching you. But if you make it through, there's no reason you can't work as a fully qualified doctor."

Anne threw her arms around him in glee. "Thank you," she said, sniffing back tears.

"Thank me by becoming the best damn doctor in all of Scotland," he replied. If Anne started weeping, he might not be able to bring himself to leave.

"I have something for you, too," Anne said, and thrust a folded piece of paper into his hands.

He frowned down at it, taking in the hand-drawn map with tiny stars scattered across Europe. "What is this?"

"Mama and I worked it out. It's all possible rips in the time veil for the next fifty years, for each of us. As close as we could get, anyway. It might not work, but at least this way there's a chance we'll see each other again."

Henry swallowed over the lump in his throat and hugged his sister one last time. Lydia was waiting behind Anne, while George checked his watch to make sure they were still on time. Their scheduled train would get them to Manchester with plenty of time to make it to the time veil, but that didn't mean they could dawdle.

He gave his mother a tight hug. "I love you, Ma," he whispered.

She let out a soft, choking sob. "I love you, too. And I want you to know—I understand."

Henry let her go and wiped at a stray tear. "Thank you." He glanced at the door, where Shepard waited expectantly with George. "And I see what Shepard is to you," he added quietly. "You should be happy, Ma. Maggie and Annie would understand."

Lydia's eyes widened. "I—that would—people would talk, Henry."

"They would. But you'd be happy."

She looked over her shoulder and then back at Henry, nodding. "Thank you. You grew into a good man, you know. Your father would be proud."

Henry nodded in turn and brushed one last kiss to her cheek.

He had a train to catch.

Chapter Thirty-Two

George sat silently next to him as the train sped through the countryside, uncharacteristically silent. They were drawing near to Manchester, well out of Scotland by now.

"Everything all right?" Henry asked, although his own nerves were jangling. The plan *should* work—he'd gotten back to his time using the same basic method—but that didn't mean it was foolproof. He could very well end up in the wrong year, or decade, or century, and fixing that would be next to impossible, even with Anne's map. Then he would be trapped without Daphne or his family, and he didn't much fancy that. Henry was not, at his core, an adventurer.

"I'll miss you, is all," George said, gaze firmly on the window. "I know why you're leaving, and I understand, but it feels like I'm losing another family member."

"I—"

"Don't," George said tightly. "You're not going to stay, and anyway, I won't let you. Doesn't mean I don't hate it, though."

"I'll miss you," Henry offered, feeling like it wasn't enough. He too was losing a brother, and the hope of seeing Daphne again didn't quite quash the wave of sadness that brought on.

But a longer, heartfelt goodbye was not in the cards, as the train began to slow. "There's no stop here, is there?" Henry asked, peering out.

"No, and we're not to Manchester yet, either," George agreed. He stood behind Henry, both of them craning their necks to try and see down to the engine. The countryside surrounding them was still pastoral, not Manchester's grimly imposing redbrick factories and warehouses.

"Excuse me, sir, but why have we stopped?" George asked a conductor who was making his way down the train, looking harried.

The man sighed heavily. "There's a tree down on the line. We'll have to move it before we can start again."

Henry's stomach jolted. "No, that can't—we need to go. I must be in Manchester, soon."

The conductor shrugged. "We'll be on our way as soon as that tree is moved, sir. But not before."

Henry looked at George pleadingly, and his friend nodded. "Then we get off. We're, what, a half an hour from Manchester by train? There must be a mail coach headed that way. We just have to find it and convince them to go . . . fast. Very fast," George said.

Henry checked his watch. They had an hour and a half until the portal opened, which he'd felt was cutting it too fine in the first place, but his mother had asked him to stay one last night at home, and he hadn't been willing to deny her that.

But now he was looking at the possibility of never seeing Daphne again, and his heart threatened to break all over again at the thought. "We've no time to waste, then." Henry grabbed the backpack from the twenty-first century and headed for the train carriage's door. The conductor was busy pacifying a middle-aged couple who did not like stopping on journeys, "on account of my wife's nerves," and didn't so much as spare them a glance as Henry and George hopped down off the train into the middle of a field.

George's boots hit the ground behind him, and Henry immediately turned around. "Which way, do you think?"

George looked around and nodded to his right. "Over there. See that ridge right at the end of the field? Looks to be a lane up there. If someone's going toward town, we should be able to spot them there."

Personally, Henry felt like this was a fairly thin plan, but then again, he didn't have much choice. There was no way the train would make it to Manchester on time, so this was his only remaining hope.

It felt as though reaching the lane took forever, and once they made it, his heart sank further. It was hardly even a lane, much less a road, and barely more than a dirt track that connected farm fields to one another. It appeared to be utterly deserted, and now Henry's fear reached full-blown panic.

"What now?" he insisted, as though George had a magical answer he had been keeping from Henry all this time.

As if a higher power heard him, the faint sound of horse hooves on dry, packed earth and the rattle of wagon wheels answered. A farmer driving a cart rose over a small hill farther down the lane, trundling steadily forward.

Henry didn't wait for George and broke into a run. "Sir, I have—I need to beg a favor," Henry called.

The man took in their clothes, rather out of place—if mussed—for a mostly deserted field. "You gentlemen look to be lost," the farmer observed.

"My friend needs your horse," George said bluntly. "We'll pay you."

The farmer looked puzzled. "But I need her to pull the cart."

"That much we can see," George replied. "But—"

"But if I don't make it to Manchester in the next" Henry checked his pocket watch and experienced yet another unpleasant stomach lurch—"seventy-five minutes, I'll never see the woman I love again."

"Well, now, I don't know if I see how that's possible. If she's in Manchester now, won't she be in seventy-five minutes?"

"She's not there," Henry nearly yelled, keeping leash of his fear at the last minute. "She's—" He looked to George, utterly unprepared to come up with a plausible lie.

"She's in London, but his train to London leaves in an hour. And she won't be there tomorrow, when the next train arrives."

The farmer nodded slowly. Too slowly, in Henry's increasingly desperate opinion. "Well, that I can understand. My mare here isn't a racehorse, though. She's young, but she's not—"

"She'll suffice, I'm sure," Henry said. "And as he said, we'll pay you."

"And I'll pick her up in Manchester and bring her back this evening," George added.

The farmer agreed and carefully, painstakingly, climbed down. "Did you need help unhooking her?" he offered.

"It's quite all right. We can manage," George said affably.

"Thank you. I owe you one," Henry said quietly as they got to work. His heart was still racing and his pocket watch was ticking so loudly it felt like a thunderclap, or maybe that was just his heart as well.

"Tough for me to collect, what with you going almost two centuries into the future and all," George said wryly. He smiled sadly at Henry and tossed him the reins.

Henry was a fair horseman, although bareback had never been quite his forte. But needs must, so Henry pulled his best friend into a tight hug. "Thank you," he said again. "I'll miss you."

"I'll miss you too, but I won't if you don't get going and miss your chance," George said. He patted Henry on the back and stepped away.

Henry mounted the horse with a quick assist from the fence nearby and tipped his hat in thanks to the farmer.

And then, with one last look, he was off.

◆ ◆ ◆

Henry's muscles ached from holding himself on the horse, who was, as the farmer had said, fast but not about to win any races. Still, he found himself in the outskirts of Manchester in good time, although the horse was beginning to flag.

He slowed her to a steady trot as the traffic thickened, and if possible, his nerves got worse. He had to make it to a cemetery on the eastern side of the city, but he hadn't counted on the streets being clogged with workers on their way home from shifts at the factory. Soon the trot slowed to a walk and he wove between carriages as carefully as he could, urging the horse—clearly not at ease with city traffic—forward.

He had memorized the turns to the cemetery from the train station, but that did not help as much as he would have liked, given that he was now coming from an entirely different direction. He hailed a pedestrian and asked for directions to the cemetery, trying to be polite while his anxiety mounted.

"Saint Mary's? Not too far from here, no," the old woman replied. "Just up thataway a little."

"Which road, ma'am?"

She started a long, discursive explanation of the road (Saint Mary's Avenue) followed by which direction to turn at the top of the hill (left), along with several completely unrelated asides about her health (poor), her knee (always aching), and her daughter-in-law (ungrateful, and also pregnant). Henry was barely holding a scream back with his teeth when she finished and he could head on, the streams of carriages, hacks, and pedestrians finally thinning as he approached the hill. Henry checked his watch once more, realizing with dawning horror that he had only minutes to spare, and quite a hill for the horse to climb.

"Come on, girl," he urged, kicking her flanks. "One last run."

Surprisingly, she obeyed, once more speeding up to a canter. Henry turned at the gate into the cemetery, hopping down from the horse without bothering to hobble her. Either George would find her and pay the farmer for his generosity, or else someone would steal her and George would be out a bit more money, but now was not the time for worrying about that, because up ahead, he saw a twisting, turning shimmer.

Henry broke into a dead sprint, hoping he wouldn't miss it, not sure how long the veil would even stay open. He threw one look over his shoulder as he approached, to take a last look at his century, and then plunged straight into it.

His stomach dropped, and everything went dark.

Chapter Thirty-Three

Daphne hitched the grocery bag higher on her shoulder, the first few leaves of autumn crunching under her feet. In the year since Henry had left, she and Ellie had regressed to their diets of frozen pizzas and takeout, but Daphne did make an attempt to cook a real meal on one of her days off. Ellie always liked coming back from an exhausting shift in the ER to find something that didn't just have plastic ripped off, and Daphne was going to do her best to keep that going.

If she couldn't have Henry, she could at least keep his memory close. That was what she'd been telling herself for the last six months, once she finally made herself admit he wasn't coming back. It wasn't that she thought there would be an easy way for him to get back, but rather that a part of her had insisted on hoping that, against all evidence, he might figure something out.

For the first three months he was gone, everyone coddled her. Even when she gave them her news and they were varying levels of sad (Brittany, Michelle), smug because he knew it (Vibol), and betrayed (Ellie), they let her nurse her broken heart without comment. After it had been six months, Ellie started gently nudging her to stop moping all the time, and three months after *that*, Vibol and Michelle staged an intervention with Brittany's help. They cared, she knew that, and she knew that if the tables had been turned and it was one of them who could barely think about the future, she would have done the same. So she pulled herself out of the funk as best she could, and started putting one foot in front of the other.

Daphne had even agreed to go on a date, although she didn't think her friends expected much to come of it. He was a friend of Michelle's cousin—her real cousin—doing a postdoc in epidemiology and public health at the University of Minnesota. He was handsome and sweet, and they managed to find enough to talk about to make it through drinks and dinner, but in the end, she just couldn't bring herself to do anything but give him a hug and tell him she'd had a nice time. He didn't call her after either, so at least she didn't feel guilty or anything. He would be fine, and so would she. Eventually.

The moon peeked out from behind a white, fluffy cloud, and Daphne felt the familiar-but-now-slightly-muted stab of loss when she saw it. The moon had been out in the daytime when she first met Henry too, and while that wasn't uncommon, it still hurt to see sometimes. Like a flash of a memory when she least expected it.

She turned the corner, the familiar cream-colored brick of their building up ahead. Her new clinic was farther away than the hospital, but close enough that she hadn't felt like she needed to move. Which was good, because without Henry, she definitely needed her friends close by.

Daphne shuffled her feet through an eddy of fallen leaves like a kid, reminding herself that finding joy in small things was important, even if she was starting to realize her life would always feel like it had one big gaping hole in it.

Out of the corner of her eye, she saw a man leaning back against the building as if waiting for someone, his frame achingly familiar. She kept her gaze down, because she was used to this, unfortunately. For months after Henry left, she saw him *everywhere*: at the clinic, in line to catch the bus, waiting outside a movie theater. It happened less often now, but maybe that was just because she had a system—she saw a tall, dark-haired white man with broad shoulders and her eyes would immediately go unfocused, darting away before her heart had a chance to leap.

The man straightened as she approached, and she tensed her stomach, anticipating the unpleasant lurch that would happen when he spoke to her to ask for directions somewhere and she had to force herself to look at him and her brain would do the *it's him, oh, no wait, it isn't* dance. Daphne started rummaging through her purse for her keys, hoping he would get the *don't talk to me* hint.

"Daphne?" a voice with a deep Scottish lilt asked, and Daphne froze on the spot, eyes still glued to the inside of her purse because—no. It wasn't him. It couldn't be, because she had worked *so hard* to remind herself it would never be him, and she couldn't afford to hope that she might have been wrong. "Aren't you a sight for sore eyes."

She dropped the grocery bag and food went everywhere. Half a dozen oranges bounce-jiggled on the pavement, and a bag of granola split open upon impact, spilling out a small mountain of oats. A can of tomato soup rolled steadily across the sidewalk, coming to a stop next to a foot in an old-fashioned leather boot.

Slowly, Daphne dragged her eyes up, unable to breathe. Wool pants gave way to a white shirt, which gave way to a face she'd dreamed of so often she still half wondered if she was hallucinating. "No," she whispered.

Henry grinned, as cocky as ever. "Oh, yes. I'm back, my lady."

Daphne dropped her purse on top of the groceries and threw her arms around his neck, dragging his scent into her lungs, feeling the warmth of his chest against hers. He was so solid, so warm, so *real* that tears started pricking at the corners of her eyes. "How?" she finally asked in a strangled voice.

Henry pulled back just far enough to look into her eyes. "I'll tell ye that later," he said, and it wasn't until he kissed her that she knew, really knew, that this was real, because even in her dreams, he never quite kissed her like that.

Henry was, however improbably, back.

◆ ◆ ◆

ER Doc (And the Traitor Daphne Griffin) Group Chat

Daphne

Everyone down to my place
911
Nobody's hurt
Still
911

Brittany

Girl STOP double texting, it's so annoying
And be right there

Vibol

Stop double texting says the double texter

Michelle

Are you okay Daph?

Daphne

Yes it's a good 911

Ellie

There's no such thing as a good 911 sweetie

Vibol

Ellie's got a point

Daphne

WILL YOU ALL SHUT UP AND COME DOWN TO MY PLACE?

Ellie

*Our
You mean our place

Vibol

I take her silence to mean she's annoyed with us

Michelle

Says the man who has never been silent IN HIS LIFE

Brittany

Am I the only one even in the building other than Daph? Why am I the only one in the elevator

Ellie

I'm up in Vibol and Michelle's apartment and they're taking F O R E V E R to get their shoes on

Michelle

Note: Vibol is taking forever, I'm ready

Vibol

The fact that none of y'all untie your damn shoes is barbaric

Daphne grinned down at her phone and clicked it off. "They'll be here any minute now," she said. She couldn't stand still and kept pacing back and forth, looking at his back while he dug out the clothing he had left behind from the bottom of her closet. Everyone had kept telling her to donate his stuff as a way of symbolically moving on, but Daphne hadn't been able to bring herself to part with them yet. As it turned out, she was glad she'd held on to them.

"Thank you," he murmured, dropping the bundle of clothes onto her bed.

"For what?" Daphne asked, turning her head slightly to give him a quick kiss.

"For not falling in love with someone else while I was gone," Henry said wryly.

"I could say the same to you," Daphne replied.

Henry paused, considering. "I was actually only gone three months."

"It was a year and three months," Daphne replied.

"For you, yes. But for me, I was only back from the solstice to the equinox."

"Was that enough time with your family?"

"It wasn't, but it also was," Henry said wistfully. "They understood why I left, at least. And it was my best chance to get back to you."

Daphne threw her arms around his neck and hugged him, what he'd given up washing over her. "Thank you."

Daphne left her bedroom at the sound of the doorknob. Brittany strode in, looking around. "You said you weren't hurt, but I assume you like, need help moving something large?"

"If that were what she needed, she'd just have called me," Vibol said from behind her.

"No, she would have called me, dummy. I'm her roommate." Ellie toed her shoes off and cocked her head as she looked around, puzzled.

"Hey, don't call him *dummy*. Only I get to do that," Michelle chided. "Is it another IKEA bookcase?"

"That would be an egregious misuse of a 911 text," Brittany pointed out.

Vibol was already rummaging through their cupboard of snacks. "Did you get the popcorn from Costco, El?"

"Bottom shelf, on the left," she replied. "But seriously, Daph, what's wrong?"

"Nothing's wrong—"

"You better not be switching specialties again," Vibol said, opening the popcorn and handing it over to Ellie.

"Yeah, you're really happy where you are. It's a good fit," Ellie added.

"I don't mean like that—I mean I can't take her changing programs again."

"It literally has nothing to do with you," Michelle argued.

"Does anyone want to hear what my news is, or are you just going to roast me for a while?"

"They're going to roast you for a bit, yeah," Brittany said. She boosted herself up to sit on the edge of the counter and reached over to grab a handful of popcorn from Ellie.

"Maybe this will give you guys something else to argue about," Henry said, emerging from Daphne's room in jeans and a long-sleeved shirt that fit so perfectly that Daphne abruptly wanted her friends to all leave immediately.

Everyone else's reactions were just as drastic, if slightly less horny. Ellie dropped the popcorn on the ground while Vibol yelled and started choking, which made Michelle rush to his side to pat his back while also saying "No way no way no FUCKING way" over and over again. Only Brittany managed to swing herself down and run to hug him, squealing loudly the whole way.

"How the fuck did this happen?" Vibol finally said, chugging a glass of water.

"I time-traveled," Henry said with a grin.

"Obviously. But we thought there wasn't a way to manage that for another seven years?"

"That's because we were looking at direct ones from here to Edinburgh, not from somewhere else in Britain to anywhere on the North American continent," Henry replied. "My mother and sister managed to find one from Manchester to Miami, thanks to Ellie's equation."

"How'd you get from Miami to here, though?" Michelle asked.

"I found a lovely woman who was willing to spot me the bus fare, so long as I agreed to pay her back eventually."

"It helps to have a face like that," Ellie said.

"Don't I know it," Vibol added. "How long are you here for?"

Henry reached for Daphne and threaded his fingers through hers. "For good. If she'll have me."

"Oh, she'll have you, all right," Ellie muttered.

"She's been pining after you. We were getting worried," Brittany added.

Vibol set his glass down. "Not like, worried-worried. But concerned worried."

Henry tugged Daphne close and let her hand drop so he could wrap his arm around her shoulders, and she snuggled in tighter. It felt so unbelievably good to hold him again; she wasn't sure if she'd ever be able to stop touching him.

Henry nuzzled the top of her head. "Vibol said you switched specialties. When did that happen?"

"Right after you left," Daphne said. "You asked me to, and I didn't think I'd see you ever again, so it felt like . . . the right thing to do."

"We made sure she wasn't doing it just for you, though," Ellie interjected.

"Yeah, we had like, fifteen interventions before she went through with it," Vibol added.

"Correction: We had one intervention, and then Ellie had fourteen more," Brittany said.

Ellie sniffed. "I just wanted to make sure she was doing it for the right reasons."

"What are the 'right reasons'?" Henry asked.

"To make myself happy, and not you," Daphne explained.

"And you all are satisfied she did it for the right reasons?"

"She's been happier than I've ever seen her, except for when she's moping about you," Ellie said.

Daphne beamed. "I'm at a family practice clinic now. I get to have actual conversations with patients, not just ask them what happened and quick-order some tests."

"Hey, some of us *like* getting to do that," Vibol protested.

"That's because you have absolutely no bedside manner," Michelle said, patting his hand.

"Exactly," Vibol said. "But what do you think you'll do, Henry?"

"Pretty sure he's going to become a kept man," Brittany said.

"A . . . kept . . . man?" he asked.

"Means I pay for everything," Daphne explained with a grin. "Which is fine, but you will need to cook dinner."

"That's what I was thinking, actually. Not the kept-man thing, but—cooking. Professionally. It'll take some time to get to the level I need to be at, but I think I'd enjoy it."

"Yes, chef," Brittany said with a salute, and at his blank look, she sighed and shook her head, muttering about needing to keep up his television education under her breath.

"I think that's brilliant," Daphne said, leaning over to kiss him while their friends groaned theatrically.

"Oooh, hey, now that you're back, can you cook for us again? As practice for your future career?" Michelle asked excitedly.

"I'd love to," Henry said. "Mac and cheese?"

"The stuff from the box?" Ellie asked, her eyebrows raising.

"It's what I missed most," Henry confessed sheepishly.

"I think we've got a box somewhere," Ellie said.

"I've got two up in my apartment," Brittany added.

Henry smiled so broadly Daphne's own cheeks ached. "Then I'll get the water boiling," he announced.

Chapter Thirty-Four

One year later

Daphne woke to the usual sound of dishes clattering softly in the kitchen and the unmistakable scent of bacon. She rolled out of bed and pulled on a sweatshirt, padding out into the kitchen, where Henry was halfway into waffles, bacon, and what appeared to be eggs Benedict.

"Smells delicious," she said, wrapping her arms around his waist.

"Morning," he said, and craned his neck to kiss her. The angle was off and the kiss was brief, but it still made her stomach sizzle like a pat of butter dropped onto a hot pan. "Everyone's off this morning, so they're coming over for breakfast."

"Weren't you going to wake me?"

"You were up late last night on the phone with your patient. Figured you would need more sleep, but I would have woken you before they showed up."

Daphne's patient was a new mom, struggling with infant twins who had spiked their first-ever fever. She was stressed and overwhelmed, and when Daphne saw the panicked message the mother had sent at 11:00 p.m., she knew she needed to call her back immediately. It had taken longer than she thought to calm her down, but she was glad she'd taken the time because in the end, the patient had sounded exhausted but relieved. Next year she'd finally be done with her residency, just one year behind her friends, and she and Henry had already started talking about what the future might look like for them. There were a few clinics in the Twin Cities that she thought might be a good fit—give her the chance to actually help people while still providing enough variety to keep her interested each day. They were working on a way to visit Henry's family too, although that would have to involve multiple portals and a not-insignificant amount of studying by Daphne to be prepared for (as she still insisted on calling it, mostly because it annoyed Henry) "Olden Times."

"What's the menu today?" Brittany asked, walking in with Ellie from their apartment across the hall, both of them still in their pajamas. "Smells good."

Henry started explaining what he'd made, going off on a tangent with Ellie about a particular technique he'd recently learned for poaching eggs. One of Brittany's sketchy exes had gotten him some forged identification so he could find work. His new job as a line cook meant he had terrible hours, but he was thriving; that much Daphne could see.

Pretty soon Vibol and Michelle arrived. Daphne buzzed them up, and when they walked in, it felt like everything was finally in place. Henry looked up from the stove and caught her eye, smiling warmly, like he knew what she was thinking.

Here, right now? Everything was perfect.

Acknowledgments

First, to any reader who caught the factual errors in my book: I apologize. In particular, the most egregious error (and one I made deliberately) is that the Married Women's Property Act in Britain was, in fact, passed in 1882, yet Maggie argues against getting married because she wants to retain the rights to her property in 1885. The reason for the misalignment between historical fact and this book is simple: Henry had to be from 1885 because that's when *Back to the Future Part III* takes place. In order for him to be worried about the family business, there needed to be more of a question about who could run it, and in order for *that* to happen, I needed to bump the Married Women's Property Act by a few years. Additionally, there were a handful of women doctors by 1885, but I'll be honest: Henry repeatedly not believing Daphne was a doctor made me laugh. When forced to choose between "being accurate" and "making a joke," I generally lean toward the latter, so how about we pretend he was just very thickheaded about women in medicine in general. I hope, since this book also involves time travel via portals influenced by ley lines, phases of the moon, and astrology signs, you can forgive my dedication to jokes and *Back to the Future* despite the inaccuracies (on these and any other mistakes I may have made).

Next, every book is both a lonely, solitary adventure and a group project, and a lot (a lot) of people helped get this one out into the world and deserve a whole lot of credit.

To my agent, Kimberly Brower: Thank you for taking me on as a client and believing in this wild little book I pitched right at the end of a Zoom meeting. Thank you to everyone at Montlake, particularly Maria Gomez for seeing the potential in my pitch, and Mackenzie Walton for helping me shape it into the story I knew it could be.

An enormous thank-you to Jenna Levine, Katie Shepard, and Thea Guanzon for encouraging me to run with "what if a guy time-traveled and also looked like Robb Stark" as a viable plot, and to Erin, Brit, and Chash for listening to me whine whenever I was stuck. Lindsey, I love you and I cannot thank you enough for your support over this past year. Matt and Hailey, our book club helped keep me sane while writing this, so thank you for your patience whenever I couldn't make it due to deadlines. Hännah and Britt, as always, you're the best friends a girl can ask for.

To everyone who served as a resource about medicine, doctors, and "plausible diagnoses that could make someone think they were from the past": I sincerely appreciate it, and I hope you all enjoy finding your names in the cast of characters at the hospital.

Thank you also to my readers, reviewers, and anyone who has ever liked my books enough to mention them on social media. I am able to write because of you, and I am forever grateful.

I have somehow managed to publish three books now, and I could not have done so without the support of my family (Mom, Dad, and the Boston Contingent) and my in-laws (there's far too many of you to list, but an extra-big thank-you to you guys for providing childcare when I struggled to balance everything). Tdee Muay and Tdee Bee, I love you more than you can possibly imagine, and I cannot believe how much you've grown in the past few years.

Lastly, to my husband: Thank you for loving me, always making me laugh, and loving *Back to the Future* so much that it gave me an idea for a book. I hope you like this one.

About the Author

Elizabeth Davis is the author of *The Player Next Door* and *I Love You, I Hate You*, as well as numerous novellas and short stories. She is a full-time nerd who likes cold weather, coffee, and public television. (She is also a lot cooler than that sounds.) Born and raised in suburban Milwaukee, Elizabeth now lives in Minneapolis, Minnesota, with her husband and two children. For more information, visit www.elizabeth-davisromance.com.